MW00959227

Amy Cross is the author of more than 250 horror, paranormal, fantasy and thriller novels.

Amy Cross

This edition
first published by Blackwych Books Ltd
United Kingdom, 2024

Copyright © 2024 Blackwych Books Ltd

All rights reserved. This book is a work of fiction.
Names, characters, places, incidents and businesses are
the product of the author's imagination or are
used fictitiously. Any resemblance to actual persons,
living or dead, or to actual events or locations,
is entirely coincidental.

Also available in e-book format.

www.amycross.com
www.blackwychbooks.com

CONTENTS

BEN

CHAPTER ONE

SHE UNBUCKLED THE SEAT belt, opened the
car door and stepped out onto a rough gravel
driveway. A gentle breeze was blowing all around,
rustling the treetops, but the house itself stood still
and dark and silent.

Almost defiantly so.

For a few seconds, Julia Parker could only
stand and watch the windows. With no lights on
inside, the house looked desolate and a little dismal,
half abandoned, and the windows only reflected a
cold view of the forest. Although she wasn't really
sure what she was looking *for*, Julia continued to
stare as if she expected to spot some sign of
movement, which she knew should be impossible –
after all, the guy had clearly stated that the key was
in a box next to the front door and that the entire
stay was going to be self service.

That was the whole point.

Self service.

No contact with anyone.

After a moment, realizing that she'd somehow forgotten to breathe, Julia swallowed hard, and then she heard the faintest clicking sound coming from the car's back seat.

Oh yeah.

Right.

She turned and looked down, and she immediately saw Henry's fearful eyes staring back up at her.

"It's okay," she said, finally breaking the silence as she removed her baseball cap. Then she remembered to smile, to try to pretend that everything was just fine. "We're here. You can get out now."

She waited, but the boy merely continued to watch her.

"We're here," she said again. "Henry, did you hear me? You can get out of the car now. Don't you want to stretch your legs?"

Again she waited – and again he made no move.

Realizing that she needed to prompt him a little, she crunched her way across the gravel and grabbed the handle, pulling the door open. Once more, she forgot to smile at first, only remembering when it was a fraction of a second too late to be entirely convincing.

The smile was only for the outside. On the inside, it was completely irrelevant.

"Hey," she continued. "Come on. Time to get out and move around a little."

Now it was Henry's turn to hesitate, before finally he unfastened his own seat belt and slowly swung his legs out, and then he got to his feet and immediately looked straight over at the house.

"It's going to be fun," Julia told him, almost putting a hand on his shoulder – almost, but not quite. "I know it's... I know it looks a little gloomy, but it's only for a few days, only until..."

Her voice trailed off.

"Do you want to help me carry a couple of bags in?" she asked, heading around to the rear of the car and struggling for a moment to get the boot open. "I could really *use* some help and -"

Before she could finish, she looked into the boot and saw that the two holdall bags were only taking up a small part of the space – the rest of the space was filled with various types of rope, some clear plastic bags containing needles and bundles of zip-ties. She stared at them all for a moment, before grabbing one of the holdalls and stepping back around to the door. Thrusting the bag into Henry's hands, she realized that she should probably not let him see exactly what was in the boot.

No need to scare him.

"Are you going to be okay with this?" she

asked. "It's not too heavy for you, is it?"

He felt the weight of the bag for a moment before shaking his head.

"There's a box next to the front door," she continued. "It's got the key in it. The code is eight two nine four. Do you want to go and get the place opened up for us?"

Henry stared up at her almost as if he hadn't even heard the request.

"Go on," she added. "Eight two nine four."

Turning, he slowly and clearly reluctantly began to carry the holdall toward the house. His unenthusiastic steps crunched on the gravel as he walked past the front of the car.

"Eight two nine four!" she called after him. "Remember that. I'll be right behind you."

She watched him go for a few seconds longer, and then she stepped around to the boot and pulled out the second holdall bag. As she did so, she saw the sets of handcuffs; she stared at them for a moment and then, relieved that she hadn't needed them so far, she slammed the boot shut.

CHAPTER TWO

"MAN, IT'S COLD IN here," she said ninety seconds later, as she stepped into the house's hallway and her boots bumped loudly against the bare wooden floorboards. "I think I can almost see my breath."

Setting the holdall down on a wooden chair just inside the door, she spotted a switch on the wall and gave it a flick. A dusty bulb flickered to life above, scaring away a spider and casting just enough light to allow Julia to see that the hallway was long and narrow, with thick wooden panels on the walls and precious little decoration save for a fairly small framed drawing of the house itself on one side.

A set of stairs ran up to the top floor, which looked dark and slightly menacing. There was something rather unwelcoming about the place, but after a moment Julia realized that the most disconcerting thing of all was the utter silence.

"Henry?"

She waited, and for a fraction of a second she worried that he might have gone straight through the house and run out the other side, but a moment later he stepped partially into view in the farthest doorway.

He was st ill clutching the holdall.

"It's okay, you can put that down now," she told him.

Staring back at her, he seemed uncertain.

"The room at the top of the stairs on the right is for you," she continued. "I saw photos online. There should be a nice single bed in there for you, and a set of drawers. You can take the things out of the bag and put them in, if you like. They should fit you."

She waited for him to go upstairs, but already she could tell that he was deeply suspicious. All along, even while planning the trip, she'd told herself that everything was going to be alright once they reached the house, that Henry would understand why he had to go with her and that he'd come to realize that she was only trying to help and that he might even start to relax a little and that he'd certainly at least cooperate a little more.

Once they reached the house.

Now, however, she felt as if the opposite

was happening, as if reaching the house was only making him more scared. She had to admit that the place wasn't nearly as homely and warm-looking as if had appeared in all the photos online, but she figured that she could change that. She knew there was a real fireplace and that some logs had been left, and she supposed that they might both feel better once they'd had something to eat and the place was filled with the smell of food.

She also knew that there was a television *and* a video game console, so Henry should be able to amuse himself while they waited things out.

Right now, however, he was simply standing in that doorway and clutching the holdall and staring back at her. The place was so dark and gloomy that he seemed almost to be in danger of sinking back out of sight without even moving a muscle.

"Come on," she said finally, stepping over to the stairs and patting the handrail, almost as if she was trying to lure a dog over. "Why don't you go up and take a look around and I'll... I'll get things sorted out down here. Sound good?"

He hesitated for a moment longer, before finally shuffling forward and making his way over to join her. He slipped past without touching her and then he began to walk up the stairs, a couple of which creaked and complained a little under the weight of his scuffed trainers.

Watching him going up toward the landing, Julia tried to think of something she could say that might make him feel better, or that might at least put him slightly more at ease. She'd assumed that eventually she *would* be able to talk to him, yet so far no words were coming to mind and she was starting to worry that nothing was ever going to fill the silence. And as she watched the top of his head disappearing into the murky unlit space above, she felt a sliver of disgust running through her belly as her thoughts threatened to stray again, as she almost thought about the one thing she'd promised herself she couldn't think about.

Not now.

Not until this – whatever *this* was – had ended.

"The one on the right," she said again as she saw that he was almost at the top. Reaching up, she absent-mindedly fiddled with her necklace. "The one with the single bed. That's yours. There's a set of drawers and... yeah, just make yourself at home."

He glanced back down at her.

"It's going to be okay," she added, trying to sound as reassuring as possible. "I know that might seem unlikely right now, but I promise you. I swear, everything's going to be just fine. We just have to get through the next few days."

CHAPTER THREE

SITTING AT THE LITTLE square table in the kitchen, staring at the window and watching the trees on the far side of the clearing, Julia finally heard the complaining creak of a step on the stairs. Henry was making his way back down.

"I'm in here," she said, breaking the silence of the room.

She waited.

The silence began to settle again.

"Henry? I'm in the kitchen."

Although part of her worried that he might try to run, a few seconds later she heard a faint shuffling sound coming from the hallway. She looked over at the door and saw a hint of something moving, reflected in a pane of glass, and she realized that the boy was making his way through to join her.

Good.

So far he was being very compliant.

Obviously he'd learned.

"Hey there," she said as soon as he stepped into view. She managed to smile a little more quickly this time, pretending to be a little more spontaneous. "How's the room."

"It's... okay," he said softly – so softly that anyone a little further away wouldn't have been able to hear him at all.

"There's a television in the living room," she told him. "And a games console. You like to play games, don't you?"

He stared back at her as if he was scared of giving the wrong answer, but finally he nodded.

"Before you go and check that out," she continued, "can you come and sit down for a moment?"

He remained in the doorway, and she could tell now that his shoulders were tense, as if he was ready to run at any moment.

"It's just about the service station," she added, trying to reassure him. "I thought we should talk about what happened at the service station earlier."

Again he failed to really respond in any way.

"I'm sorry if I scared you," she went on. "I'm sure I must have done. I just got a little... upset for a few minutes and I suppose I didn't handle it very well, but that's all my own fault. You mustn't blame yourself."

As she waited for him to respond, she realized that he was barely daring to move at all. All things considered, he looked almost like a painting rather than a real boy, and she couldn't help but feel that all his stillness and silence was merely a precursor to some sudden burst of energy that might come if he tried to escape.

When he tried to escape.

Then again, he seemed very much like a follower rather than a leader. Even at the age of just ten years old, his lack of initiative was striking.

"I know people were giving me funny looks," she admitted. "I swore I wouldn't let anything like that happen, but as we were sitting there... I just want you to know that nothing like that is every going to happen again. It'll probably take some time before you realize you can trust me, but... you *can* trust me. Everything I'm doing, Henry, is to protect you. To keep you one hundred per cent safe from... well, from everything. You know that, don't you?"

Although she knew he wasn't likely to give her an answer one way or another, she still left a momentary pause so that he at least had a chance.

"It won't happen again," she added somewhat uncertainly. "I promise."

"Can I go and try the games now?" he asked.

As much as she wanted to keep apologizing for everything that had happened earlier at the service station, she finally realized that there was no point pushing too hard. She'd done what she could and he was only a little boy, so she figured she just needed to give him some time and space so he could get used to the unusual situation.

"Sure," she said finally, trying yet again to offer a calm and comforting smile. "Go for it. Knock yourself out."

CHAPTER FOUR

STANDING AT THE KITCHEN window, staring out at the clearing and at the trees beyond, Julia wondered just how the world could be so quiet. The wind had largely died down now and the trees looked frozen in place, but a moment later – as if to counter her thoughts on the silence of the place – she heard the faintest bumping sound coming from somewhere upstairs.

She looked at the ceiling, but already the silence had returned.

After a few seconds, hearing muffled voices coming from the front room, she turned and walked around the kitchen table. Stopping in the doorway, she listened as she realized that Henry had managed to get the television working. She couldn't tell quite what he was watching, but she assumed he was trying to get the games console hooked up. He seemed like a smart kid, albeit very quiet, and she supposed that he'd be able to get the job done sooner or later.

She turned to go back to the window, but at the last second she caught some of the words coming from the television's speaker.

"A spokesman for the department insisted that no decision about cuts have been made yet," a newsreader was explaining, "and that there will be more consultations with affected employees in the new year before -"

"Fuck," Julia muttered, turning and hurrying along the corridor in a moment of sheer blind panic.

Her footsteps banged hard on the bare wooden boards as she stormed into the front room, and sure enough she saw that Henry was sitting cross-legged and staring up at the television as the news show continued.

"In other news," a different presenter said, looking straight into the camera, "police in London continue to search for one of -"

Before the man could say another word, Julia switched the television off at the plug socket. Turning, she immediately saw the scared look on Henry's face; he knew he'd done wrong, even if she hadn't specifically told him not to watch the news.

He was no idiot.

"I'm sorry," he stammered.

"It's okay," she replied, trying to seem as if

she was still in complete control. "You just..."

Unable to quite explain herself, she looked over at the games console and saw that it didn't appear to have been touched at all. She turned to Henry again and realized that he had perhaps been deliberately trying to catch a news broadcast, although she didn't want to believe that he could be quite so deceptive.

She knew she had to handle the situation carefully, however, and that she couldn't afford any repeat of her service station meltdown; a few more seconds passed, however, before she was sure she'd be able to hold everything in.

"Let's just stick to the console," she said cautiously, "and... maybe only when I'm in the room."

"I'm sorry," he said again, looking down at the floor.

"It's natural to be curious," she continued. "Just... trust me on this, okay? We -"

Suddenly she heard another faint creaking sound coming from somewhere upstairs. She looked at the ceiling; this time, when she looked down again, she saw that Henry's attention had been caught by the same thing.

"It's just... settling," she told him.

He met her gaze again.

"Old houses do that."

"Is this house old?"

"It's *quite* old," she continued, fiddling with her necklace for a moment before forcing herself to stop. "That's not the point. The point is, it's windy outside."

As those words left her mouth, she realized that she was wrong, that the wind had in fact died down. Still, she wanted to seem like she was in control.

"Don't let every little noise spook you, okay?" she added, trying yet again to seem friendly. "This is just for a few days, just until I... figure everything out."

"Then am I going to go home?"

"I just need to get it all straight in my head," she explained, "and make sure that it's safe."

"Do you mean after Jake -"

"Let's not talk about any of that," she said firmly, cutting him off before he had a chance to say anything else. "Do you remember what I told you earlier? Right before we got to the service station?"

He thought for a moment before nodding.

"Right," she added, fully aware that she sounded a little more stressed now – but unable to push all the tension from her voice, "so let's stick to that. Then everything will be okay. Okay?"

"Can I play a game now?" he asked.

"Let me just grab some tea," she replied, heading to the doorway before stopping and looking back at him.

Looking into his eyes, she saw so much fear, but she also worried that he might be plotting things behind her back. A moment later she crossed the room again and grabbed the remote control, figuring that he wouldn't be able to watch the news while that was out of his hands. She knew that she probably seemed paranoid and suspicious, but she told herself that he'd really left her with no choice.

"Just give me a few minutes to make my tea," she added, turning and carrying the remote control out of the room, "and then you can see what games are on the console. That sounds like fun, right?"

CHAPTER FIVE

ON THE TELEVISION SCREEN, an animated elf swung his sword and the big red ogre exploded into a shower of monster pieces and gold coins, which the elf immediately began to gather up.

"You're getting good at that," Julia said, glancing up from her notebook. "Are you *sure* you've never played it before?"

Still sitting cross-legged on the floor, with the controller in his hands, Henry turned and looked at her. In that moment there was so much suspicion and doubt in his expression, and so much fear, that it all seemed as if it might explode at any second.

"I haven't," he said after a moment.

"Well, you obviously have a natural aptitude for that sort of thing," she told him.

"What does... aptitude mean?"

"It means you're a fast learner. Do you play

a lot of games in general at home?"

"Sometimes."

"Do your parents buy them for you?"

"Sometimes."

"Do you play them with your friends?"

She waited, but this time he apparently saw no reason to answer. Worried that she might seem as if she was digging too much, she wondered whether she should change her tactics, yet part of her wanted to know as much as possible about what had really happened.

And why.

She stared at him for a moment longer, wondering whether – entirely by accident – she might be learning a little more about the root cause of it all. The last thing she wanted was to become some kind of amateur psychiatrist, but she couldn't help thinking back to some of the other things she'd read.

"Do you play... violent games?" she asked, trying to sound as if the question was completely innocent.

"I don't know."

"You must know."

She waited.

Silence.

"You know what a violent game is, don't you?"

He thought for a moment – and then he

shrugged.

"Do you play games that are more realistic?" she asked, nodding toward the screen. "Did you and your... friend... ever play games like that? Ones with blood and horrible things happening?"

She waited, but he seemed almost too nervous to answer.

"It's okay," she continued. "You can tell me."

"Sometimes," he admitted, and he could clearly tell now that the question was important.

"Do you play games with blood in them?" she asked, unable to help herself. "Do you play games where you have to go around killing things? Things that aren't monsters?"

He opened his mouth, as if he was about to answer, and then he looked at the screen again. His character was simply standing on a patch of grass, waiting for the next input from the controller.

Waiting to kill again.

"And do you know," she continued, "that they're *only* games? You don't ever get confused about the difference between games and real life, do you?"

He simply stared back at her, and she felt in that instant that he knew exactly what she was trying to insinuate. Not that he probably knew what the word 'insinuate' meant. Clearly his parents hadn't been encouraging him to learn lots of new words. Were they not worried at all about the eleven-plus?

"Never mind," she said finally, fully aware that she was pushing too hard. This was precisely the kind of conversation that – at the start of the whole thing – she'd sworn she wouldn't have. "Just... carry on playing. It's getting dark and soon I'll have to go and fix us something to eat." She glanced at the remote control. "You'll have to take a break from playing then, but that's okay. You need a break occasionally."

Henry continued to stare at her for several seconds, before slowly turning and getting on with the game. As he played, he was just about able to make out Julia's face reflected in the darker patches on the screen.

CHAPTER SIX

STANDING AT THE KITCHEN table, Julia looked down at the smeared baked bean juice on her plate. She hadn't even been very hungry, but she knew she should try to eat something and a simple meal had seemed like the only option. After all, she assumed that no delivery companies would be willing to venture so far out into the forest.

Not that she could risk using her phone, anyway.

Looking over at the other side of the table, she saw that Henry was slowly and unenthusiastically finished his own meal.

"Nice?" she asked.

He glanced at her, but he said nothing and after a moment he resumed the job of pushing some bread around the plate to mop up some juice.

"My mum used to be a terrible cook," Julia

continued. "She could even screw up beans on toast. The toast'd be all burned, black like charcoal, and the beans'd be boiled."

She waited, but in truth she wasn't really sure what she expected the boy to say. He certainly didn't seem very interested; he was simply focusing on the beans and she understood that this was probably his way of avoiding having to say or do anything. Looking over at the counter, she saw some old pots she'd taken out of the cupboard along with some dusty candles; she tried to think of something interesting she might mention about them, but so far she was drawing a blank.

"But burned toast has acrylamide in it," she went on. "That's not very good for you."

And then, before she had to think of anything else to say, she heard a slightly longer creaking sound coming from above. Looking up, she realized that the sound seemed to be coming from the main bedroom.

"What was that?" Henry asked.

She looked over at him again.

"Nothing."

"But -"

"It was nothing."

"But I heard -"

"I said, it was nothing," she added, a little more firmly this time. Worried that she seemed too angry, she forced a smile instead. "There's just you and me here. You know that, right?"

She waited for a reply, but he didn't seem to think that he needed to say anything.

"It's just you and me," she continued, "and that's... that's just a fact. Even if you hear weird noises, that's all they are. Noises."

He stared for a few more seconds, and then slowly he looked up at the ceiling again.

"You must be tired," she said. "I know I am. Listen, once it gets dark, we should probably both go to sleep. We both need to be rested for tomorrow."

He turned to her again.

"Why?" he asked.

"What do you mean?"

"Why do we have to be rested for tomorrow?" he continued. "Are we doing something? Are we going somewhere else?"

"We're staying here."

"Then why -"

"We just do, okay?" she added, once again trying to avoid seeming angry or frustrated. "It's just how things are. We'll... find things to do. You can play more video games if you want. Doesn't that sound like fun?"

Again she waited for a reply, and again he merely stared back at her.

"And we can go for a walk," she suggested. "Not too far. I don't want to..."

Realizing that this had perhaps been a bad suggestion, she tried to think of something else instead.

"Maybe not a walk," she said, correcting herself. "But we can go outside, just so long as we stay within eyesight of the house. I think that's the best thing. We don't want to go too far."

"How..."

Henry hesitated, as if he was worried about asking the next question.

"How far away do the nearest people live?" he managed finally.

"Why do you want to know that?" she replied, before swallowing hard.

"I don't know. I was just wondering."

"There's no need to wonder about that," she said uneasily. "I don't actually know, to be honest with you. We're a long way from a town or anywhere like that. That's all you need to know."

"But is it lots of miles?"

"It's lots and *lots* of miles," she told him, hoping to settle the discussion. "Too many to walk, that's for sure. You realize that, don't you?"

He looked down at his plate.

"Put all of that out of your mind," she continued, keen to hammer her point home. She'd been hoping she wouldn't need the cuffs at night, but now she realized that he was leaving her with no choice; she had to at least consider using them. "All that matters is that we're here, at least for the next few days. And by Monday I'm sure I'll have come up with a new plan. With something better."

"Do you think Jake -"

"Stop it!" she snapped angrily, slamming a fist against the table before instantly realizing her mistake. Sighing, she leaned back in the chair and saw the fear in Henry's eyes, but she quickly calmed herself down again – if not entirely, then enough. "I'm sorry," she added, "but I remember very specifically giving you a number of rules before we went to the service station. Do you remember them?"

He nodded.

"*All* of them?"

He nodded again.

"So let's please stick to them," she continued, beyond frustrated by her little snap of emotion. "Why don't you help me clear up in here? Then you can play games for a few more hours before bedtime. Doesn't that sound fair?"

Above them, as Julia and Henry kept their eyes fixed on one another, another wooden board let out a slow and somewhat ominous creaking sound.

CHAPTER SEVEN

"ARE YOU NEARLY DONE in there?" she called out a couple of hours later, as she heard a tap still running in the bathroom. "Henry?"

"Nearly!" he called out, and his mouth sounded full – as if, as he'd promised, he was still brushing his teeth.

"Okay, good," she muttered, standing at the bottom of the stairs and going through her coat pockets.

Muttering to herself, she pulled out a bunch of receipts. She uncrumpled them and took a look, and then she froze as she saw that one in particular was from earlier in the day:

Mulhern's Cafe and Bakery
Stensport Motorway Services

At the bottom of the piece of paper, a tiny amount of blood had been smeared across the surface. For a fraction of a second, Julia could only stare at that speck as she found herself unable to ignore her thoughts. In the very darkest recesses of her mind she was starting to remember the sensation of people staring, and the sound of feet racing closer, and the rush to the car and -

"I'm done."

Startled, she crunched the receipt back up and turned to see that Henry was up at the top of the stairs.

"I brushed my teeth," he said uncertainly, as if he was worried that he might have interrupted. "Should I go to bed now?"

"Mmm," Julia replied, nodding.

"The toilet didn't flush very well," he added. "I got it to flush eventually, but I think it might be broken."

"I'm sure it's fine."

He hesitated, as if he had something else to ask, and then – wearing the brand new pajamas Julia had picked up for him a day earlier, and which had turned out to fit quite well – he turned and shuffled off into 'his' room.

"Don't forget to leave the door open," she called out to him.

She waited for a reply, but she could already see that he'd done as instructed. In truth, he was being rather more compliant than she'd expected, although she worried slightly that he might just be lulling her into a false sense of security. Still, she felt that she'd explained things to him as well as possible, and she knew he was a smart boy. Too smart sometimes, perhaps. But not a monster.

Not so far.

At least, not obviously.

Looking again at the crumpled receipt in her hand, she briefly considered shoving it back into her pocket, before changing her mind and instead hurrying into the kitchen. She first went over to the bin and used her left foot to push down on the pedal; when she saw the remains of dinner in the black plastic bag, however, she was filled with a sudden sense of fear, so she marched to the counter.

As the idea came together in her head, she set the receipts – including the one from the service station – into an old pan and then she grabbed a box of matches. After lighting one, she lowered it into the pan and set fire to the receipts, and for the next few minutes she simply watched as they burned.

If only, she mused, everything could be destroyed so easily.

Finally, worried about setting off the smoke alarm on the other side of the room, she blew the flames out and then doused them with water from the tap, and then she placed the pan in the sink.

At the back of her thoughts, she was once

again hearing voices yelling in her memory, echoing through from earlier in the day.

"Hey, I think it's her," a man whispered. "Look! It's definitely her!"

"No," she said now through gritted teeth, even though she knew the man had been absolutely on the money. "It's all going to be okay. You just have to trust me."

She was still all alone in the kitchen as those last six words left her lips, and the room was becoming darker and darker as the last of the evening light died outside.

CHAPTER EIGHT

"RESIDENTS SAY THAT THE proposals don't go nearly far enough," the newsreader said, as Julia sat in bed watching the television on the dresser – with the volume turned down so low that even *she* almost couldn't hear it. "They're calling for more investment in infrastructure for the proposed housing development, including a new school, a police station and even a hospital. Ministers, however, insist that the area is already equipped to handle any new residents and that money *will* be made available to refit existing facilities. Local campaign groups claim that this will be too little, too late."

Hearing a creaking sound out on the landing, she looked over at the open doorway. She could see the open door leading into Henry's room, but so far she was fairly sure that he was soundly sleeping. And if he wasn't... she figured that there was no way he could get out of the house during the night, anyway.

Every door and window was sealed shut.

"Police in Kent," the newsreader continued, causing Julia to immediately look at the television again, "have made another appeal for information in the disappearance of a young boy from the Houndford area. And in a connected development, video footage from a nearby service station appears to show -"

Scrambling across the bed, she grabbed the remote control and turned the television off. After a moment, still feeling her heart pounding, she leaned back in the bed. She could feel her heart still racing and she told herself that checking the news had been a terrible mistake, yet somehow she'd been clinging to the hope that everything would just sort of... fix itself.

That there'd be no mention of her or Henry.

That no-one would bother.

That they'd be allowed to just disappear and sort themselves out.

"Stay calm," she whispered now, staring up at the ceiling.

As much as she was tempted to turn the television back on and find out a little more, the whole matter simply felt too raw. She couldn't bear the thought of hearing her own name on the news again, or Henry's name, or any of the other details about everything that had been happening. And the idea of Al showing up with some desperate plea for her to return was too much to stomach.

"It's okay," she said again, keeping her voice very low. "It's all going to be fine. Just trust the plan."

Hearing another creaking sound, she looked out at the landing.

Although she still couldn't see anyone, she climbed out of bed after a few seconds and crept quietly to the door. Once she'd looked out and seen that there was no sign of anyone on the landing, she silently made her way over to the other door, but when she looked through she saw to her relief that Henry appeared to be fast asleep. Part of her was surprised by that development, although she quickly reminded herself that she'd hurried the process on a little.

She thought back to the moment when she'd dropped the two crushed pills into the boy's baked beans and had then stirred it through. Apparently he hadn't noticed the slightly bitter taste.

Still, she knew that he was going to be fine. There would be no long-term impact; he might simply feel a little groggy in the morning.

Relieved that at least this part of her plan seemed to be working, she turned and walked back through to her room. At the last second, however she stopped and looked around at the landing again. The space was remarkably bare, with no real furniture to speak of, but that suited her just fine; the listing had shown plenty of photos of the interior and she wasn't exactly in search of creature comforts. She wanted space and emptiness and clarity.

And loneliness.

More than anything, she wanted to minimize the number of places where anything might be able to hide. Anything about the size of a young boy.

"It's going to be okay," she said to herself, barely making any sound as she almost just mouthed the words. "He trusts you. He..."

Her voice trailed off as she realized that there was no point talking to herself. So far everything was going according to plan – apart from the little wobble at the service station – and she knew that she had to avoid second-guessing herself. Checking her watch, she saw that it was more than late enough for her to sleep, and that she just needed to make sure that she was rested ready for the morning.

And ready for Henry's sleeping pills to wear off.

Making her way back into the room, she sat on the side of the bed and took a moment to take two more sleeping tablets out from the box. She stared at them for a moment, fully aware that they were her only real chance of getting any rest, but after a few seconds she began to worry.

What if somehow Henry woke up?

What if she was sleeping too deeply to hear him?

What if she needed to be alert?

Frustrated but convinced that she was making the right decision, she put the pills away and then climbed back into bed. Her mind was racing but she told herself that at least she should be able to get a little rest, and that in the morning everything would seem clearer. Rolling onto one side, she looked out at the landing and realized that although she felt exhausted, she was never going to be able to sleep.

What she *could* do, however, was use the downtime to go over the plan again and make sure that there were no loose ends.

CHAPTER NINE

SIX HOURS LATER, HAVING tossed and turned many times, Julia rolled onto her back and looked up for the umpteenth time at the dark ceiling. She'd almost managed to drift off to sleep once or twice; almost but not quite. Now her mind was racing again and she felt fairly sure that sleep was an impossible dream.

So far she'd run through the plan perhaps a hundred times, but she knew that the final stage was still a little uncertain. She hadn't quite figured out the endgame but she was sure that eventually everything was going to become settled. In many ways she'd already done the difficult part and all that remained was to finish it all off – and to prove to herself that her worst fears were entirely unfounded.

And then, as she once more flitted between

confidence and despair, she heard another and much louder creaking sound out on the landing.

This time, the sound seemed firmer and more deliberate.

She turned and looked at the open doorway, and although she felt sure that Henry was still asleep, she couldn't help but worry now that something else was up and about in the middle of the night. She stared, blinking occasionally, at the doorway for several minutes – yet she still couldn't quite convince herself that there was no cause for concern. Countless times she almost rolled over and tried again to sleep, but instead she watched the doorway for perhaps ten silent minutes until, very slowly, she saw a trace of a shadow falling across the opposite wall.

Feeling a tightening sense of dread in her chest, she continued to stare out at the landing.

Very slowly, over the next few minutes, a figure wearing some kind of black robe began to inch into view. The figure was clear and distinct yet also, in some way, a little ill-defined at the edges, but so far it most certainly appeared to be human. Its head was bowed down, keeping its features mostly out of sight, although something about the figure's gait seemed to Julia to be very much male, and after a few seconds the person stopped in the doorway as if dimly aware that it had been spotted.

Julia simply continued to stare.

Now she was starting to realize that she'd been wrong earlier, that the figure wasn't wearing a robe at all. Instead it seemed somehow to be carrying shadows, as if constantly on the verge of disappearing into a darkness within. She'd never seen anything quite so strange and she wasn't quite able to believe that it could be real, yet she also couldn't dismiss it as a mere trick of the night.

Over the next five minutes or so, the figure merely stood in place. Finally, however, it slowly turned so that it could look through into the room, and Julia saw a mournful face with a set of dark, slightly sunken eyes watching her from the gloom of lined and weathered features. As she met the figure's gaze, she was in turn struck by the immediate and absolutely certain conviction that she was looking at a dead man.

Not really knowing what else to do, she simply maintained eye contact with the man for what felt like an eternity – in truth, however, this lasted for no more than five or six minutes before slowly the figure turned and began to continue on his way, eventually but slowly shuffling out of sight. As he went, he caused yet another loose wooden board to creak slightly in the cold night air.

Julia continued to watch the door even though the house was quiet now. She wasn't sure whether the man was going to return, but eventually after perhaps half an hour she realized that her spectral visitor was clearly gone, at least for the rest of the night. Fortunately, she realized, Henry had seemingly not noticed that anything was amiss, so eventually she simply rolled over onto her other side and looked at the wall as she once again tried to get some sleep.

She didn't scream.

She didn't try to deny what she'd seen.

She just closed her eyes and resumed her long restless wait for morning.

CHAPTER TEN

BRIGHT, COLD MORNING LIGHT streamed down from a blank sky as Julia crunched her way across the dead leaves and made her way over to a stump and ax that had been left out at the rear of the house.

"How about it, Henry?" she said, struggling for a moment to pull the ax out before finally managing to twist it free.

She turned to him.

"Do you want to help me cut some wood for the fire?"

Sitting on the back steps, Henry stared at her with the same sullen and perhaps confused expression that he'd been wearing on his face all the way through breakfast.

"Isn't there some already?" he asked.

"There is, but I thought it'd be fun to chop

some ourselves."

Again she waited.

Again he stared back at her.

"Well, maybe you can just watch," she continued with a forced smile, trying to keep the conversation going. "I've never actually done this before, so I'm not sure how it's going to go."

Tucking the ax under her arm, she took her gloves from her pockets and began to slip them onto her hands.

"But how hard can it be, right?" she added, still trying to find some way to make the situation seem less hopeless. "I probably should have done some working out at the gym, though. I'm not exactly the strongest person around. That's why I thought you might be able to help."

Once her gloves were on, she realized that nothing she said was going to elicit much of a response. At the same time, she figured that she had to find some way to get them both through the day and that the only alternative would be to simply stare at the television. Then again, in that moment, the television seemed like a decent option.

"You can go and play video games if you prefer," she told him.

"Can I watch something instead?"

She opened her mouth to reply, but she hesitated as she tried to work out whether there would be any way to lock him into a particular channel. She had the remote control hidden away, and she knew that she had to make sure that Henry didn't accidentally-on-purpose find his way to a news channel.

"Is there something wrong with the video games?" she asked. "Is it not a great selection?"

"I just want to watch a show instead."

"Maybe later, with me," she continued. "I'm sure some of those other games are good, you just need to give them a chance. We've got a long day ahead of us, Henry, and we need to keep ourselves busy."

As those words left her lips, she glanced at one of the upstairs windows. For a fraction of a fraction of a second, out of the tiniest corner of her eye, she'd possibly spotted movement at one of the windows but now she saw only the reflection of the forest. The more she stared at one particular window, however, the more she realized that she wouldn't necessarily be able to see if someone was standing on the other side.

She thought back briefly to the sight of the strange man in the night. Should she, she wondered now, have been more scared?

"Where's the wood?" Henry asked suddenly.

She turned to him.

"That you're going to chop," he added. "I don't see any."

"It's over there, under that tarpaulin," she

told him, before making her way over and pulling the tarpaulin aside to reveal row upon row of stacked logs. "See? They're a bit big for the fireplace, though, so I was thinking I should cut at least half of them in two. I've never really lived out in nature like this and I kind of like the idea of doing things the old-fashioned way."

She picked up one of the larger logs and carried it back over to the stump, while glancing at Henry and seeing that he still seemed utterly impressed.

"It's pretty dangerous, though," she added, setting the log down and then examining the ax's blade. "Maybe it's better if you just watch."

Figuring that she simply needed to get on with the job, she took a step back and raised the ax up high. She felt sure that her first couple of attempts probably wouldn't go particularly smoothly, but she also told herself that she could do anything if she just put her mind to it.

"Are you serious?" she imagined Al asking. "*You're* going to try to chop wood? You'll be lucky if you don't chop your own head off."

"Whatever," she imagined herself replying.

She glanced at Henry and saw that he was watching her, and then she adjusted her grip on the ax a few more times – for no particular reason – before finally swinging it down in a desperate attempt to split the log straight down the middle.

Instead she struck the log a glancing blow, sending it flying mostly intact off the side of the side of the stump while flicking a tiny sliver up into the air and almost getting that sliver straight in her eye. And to top that off, she also felt a sharp pain in her left underarm, as if she'd pulled or at least badly strained a muscle.

"Shit!" she hissed, before quickly reminding herself that she shouldn't swear in front of the boy. She looked at him and saw that he still wasn't laughing or smiling.

"It takes practice," she told him, surprised to find that she was more than a little out of breath – but also having to hide the slight pain in her arm. "I've just got to... keep doing it until I get better. You know what they say, right? Practice makes -"

Before she could finish, she heard the distant rumble of a car making its way closer along the rough road. Turning, still holding the ax, she was shocked by the sight of a large green S.U.V. bumping around the far corner and she immediately realized that she was far too late to do anything to prevent the arrival of this visitor.

"Get inside!" she barked at Henry before turning to look at him as she felt a rush of panic in her chest. "Now! For fuck's sake, get out of sight!"

CHAPTER ELEVEN

THE AX SWUNG DOWN, perfectly splitting the log so that the two halves toppled cleanly over either side of the stump.

"It takes a lot of practice, really," Piotr said with a smile as he held the ax back out toward her. "Don't get too disillusioned that you didn't manage it on your first try. I've been doing this since I was a kid."

Although she opened her mouth to reply, for a few seconds Julia really wasn't sure what to say. Since Piotr's arrival just a few minutes earlier and his emergence from the S.U.V., everything had been a bit of a blur and she'd barely been able to protest at the intrusion. Now, however, she felt as if her mind was clearing a little. She glanced over her shoulder, just to make sure that Henry was properly out of the way, and then she turned to Piotr again.

"I'm sorry," she said cautiously, "but... who did you say you were again?"

"Piotr," he replied, repeating the one piece of information she'd actually absorbed.

He set the ax into her left hand, and then he held out his right for her to shake.

"Cymbalista," he continued. "My dad owns the house. I handle the business side of it, letting it out and all that stuff. I usually like to drop by and check on people who've rented it out, just to see how they're doing. I would've been by yesterday evening but I was out past the east meadow dealing with some beavers that've been building a dam and Dad wants me to use dynamite on them but I'm really not sure I should and..."

His voice trailed off for a moment.

Julia, meanwhile, continued to stare back at him.

"I have the dynamite in the car," he added, nodding toward the vehicle. "I can show you, if you like."

"No, that's fine," she stammered, trying to make sense of everything she'd just heard. "I... thought everything out here was automated. On the ad, it said that I'd just get the key from the little box by the front door."

"Did that not work?"

"Yeah, it worked fine."

"Great."

"So I didn't think anyone would come by," she continued, narrowing her gaze a little – and fully aware that she sounded deeply suspicious. "In fact, I specifically believed that we... that *I* wouldn't be disturbed this weekend."

"Sorry," he said, as if he still didn't quite understand her reaction.

He took a moment to look around before turning to her again.

"Sorry," he said again as the trees rustled all around the edge of the clearing. "Mrs... Jenkins, was it?"

"That's right, but why does it matter?" she replied, before checking herself just in time as she realized that she probably sounded way too nervous.

Realizing that he was looking at the house again, she turned – and she immediately felt her heart sink as she noticed that she could just about make out Henry staring from one of the windows. She looked at Piotr again and was under no doubt now that he'd also seen the boy.

"Thank you for your concern," she said cautiously, "but we're really just here for a weekend out in the countryside. We don't need anyone to check up on us or come by to make sure that we're okay. Sure, I might not be able to cut wood very well, but that was just a little bit of silliness."

"Of course," he replied, taking a step back. "I'm sorry, I guess I didn't think this through. I really didn't mean to intrude, I just thought I'd swing by since I was in the area anyway, but you're right. You came out here for a nice peaceful retreat, and that's exactly what you should be enjoying right now." He held up the palms of both hands as if in mock surrender. "Please, forgive the intrusion. It won't happen again."

Figuring that things were about to get back to normal and that the little drama was over, Julia just about managed to muster something resembling a smile.

"Thank you," she said to him. "I hope I didn't seem too harsh or ungrateful just now. It's just that Henry and I have been looking forward to this trip for a while and... we want to make the most of it."

"You won't see me again," he replied, turning and heading back toward his S.U.V., "and -"

"The toilet's broken."

Stopping, he turned to look back at the house, and Julia turned too – to see that Henry had opened the back door and was now standing at the top of the steps.

"It won't flush at all now," he continued, with a hint of a whine in his voice. He stared at Julia for a moment, then at Piotr, then at Julia again. "Do either of you know how to fix it?"

CHAPTER TWELVE

"I TOLD MY DAD not to get one of these fancy modern things," Piotr muttered, flat on his back in the bathroom upstairs as he reached behind the toilet and tried to get to one of the connectors. "There's nothing wrong with a good old – excuse the phrase – bog-standard loo, but he *had* to get one of these modern environmentally-friendly contraptions with -"

Letting out a sudden gasp, he pulled his hands down and saw blood on the side of one finger. He wiped it on the edge of his shirt before grabbing a screwdriver and immediately getting back to work.

"If this was a normal loo," he continued, "I'd have had it fixed by now. I'm sorry, Mrs. Jenkins, it really shouldn't be taking this long. I don't quite know what's wrong with it, but obviously I can't leave you without a functioning toilet, can I?"

"It's fine," Julia replied tentatively, watching him from the doorway with her arms folded across her chest. "I'm sure we can... manage."

"Without a toilet?"

"We can make do."

"Nonsense."

Checking her watch, she was entirely unable to hide a sense of frustration. More than anything, she just wanted Piotr gone so that she and Henry could get on with the day, but evidently the toilet was proving far trickier to fix than she could possibly have imagined. And as much as she wanted to offer some words of encouragement, or to insist that she and Henry could go to the toilet in the forest, she knew deep down that her best bet was probably to just suffer through a few more minutes of the handyman's attention.

And to hope that he'd be done soon.

"That's no good," he said, wincing slightly as he adjusted his angle and tried again. "I could shoot whoever designed this thing."

"If it's too much trouble," Julia replied, "then -"

"You paid an arm and a leg to rent this place," he pointed out, cutting her off. "The least you deserve is a working toilet."

"Yes, but -"

"Can't risk you leaving us a bad review."

"I won't do that, I promise," she told him, before glancing at her watch again. "I promise I'll leave a really good review. It's just that we kind of have plans."

"I can show myself out when I'm done."

"Right."

She paused again, still trying to think of some plausible and completely non-suspicious reason why she might need him to immediately leave and not come back. So far, however, she was coming up with nothing.

"I do actually know what I'm doing," he continued. "I've fixed this damn thing before. The main problem is the angle. It's so hard to really get into the gubbins from here. It's like they deliberately made it hard to fix. To be fair, I'm sure they *did* do it deliberately. They're probably in cahoots with the repairmen, making it harder for people like me to solve a problem. But I'm not letting Dad waste hundreds of quid on some idiot who'll just show up and tighten a bolt or something."

"That's very... commendable," she replied, looking over her shoulder to check that Henry was still in his room. "Out of interest, though, exactly how long do you think it's going to take?"

"Anywhere between one and sixty minutes," he sighed. "Don't worry, though. I never ever give up on a job. Once I've started, I'm like a bloodhound. I work and I work until everything's just right." He peered out from under the cistern and smiled at her. "By this afternoon, Mrs. Jenkins, you *will* have a working toilet again. But like I said, you don't need to wait around and watch me work, not if you've got things to do. Just let me get on with things here and I'm sure I'll be done soon."

Not really knowing what else to say to him, Julia could only offer a flat, frustrated smile. She knew that Piotr was just being helpful and that in ordinary circumstances she should be profusely grateful to him for fixing the toilet so attentively. The only problem was that she'd planned to avoid all conceivable variables and, well, Piotr was threatening to derail her entire plan.

"Not long now, I hope," he continued. "I think I can see the bit that's come loose. I just have to find a way to reach it." He chuckled to himself. "Isn't that always the way in life?"

CHAPTER THIRTEEN

"IF THERE ARE ANY other problems," Piotr said as he stood in the kitchen, holding the cup of tea that Julia had reluctantly felt forced to offer, "just give me a call. The number's on your booking email."

"Thank you," she replied, trying to tame the slight twitch she could feel developing on one side of her face.

They stood in silence for a moment, before Piotr slowly took a sip from his cup. The only sound was an occasional explosion coming from the television screen as Henry played another game.

"Just having a little... break from the world, then?" he continued.

"Something like that."

"And that's your son, I guess?"

She swallowed hard.

"Yes," she lied finally. "Sort -"

She stopped herself just in time. This was the kind of direct question she always found so difficult to answer.

"Yes," she said again.

"You've sure picked a fun place for your little getaway," he told her with a faint smile, having seemingly not picked up on her hesitation. "We don't get a ton of bookings here, but people who *do* come always say that they enjoy it."

"That's nice."

She was staring at the cup now, cursing herself for having filled it so close to the top. In fact, she was cursing herself for having offered it at all, and she couldn't help but wish that she'd been a little ruder. There had simply been an achingly long silence in the conversation a few minutes earlier, one that had seemed to be begging for an offer of a cup of tea or coffee. In the end, she'd made that offer on autopilot.

And now he wouldn't leave.

She'd hoped that this Piotr guy might get the message but... so far, he seemed pretty unaware of her subtle hints.

"It's great for walking," he suggested. "If you look online, you can find -"

"I'll do that," she said, interrupting him before making a point of looking at her watch.

"I'm sure you've got everything planned out

already," he muttered, taking another – rather small – sip of tea. "You don't need someone like me showing up, telling you what to do."

"Not really," she replied, hating the fact that she was having to be a little short with him now. At the same time, she really couldn't afford to be too rude, in case she aroused any suspicion. "We're just going to... enjoy nature, that sort of thing."

"You've come to the right place." He glanced at the ceiling. "Now that the toilet's working again. I guess not having a proper toilet would be a little *too* close to nature. Am I right?"

She proffered a flat smile.

"I'll get out of your hair in a minute," he added, and now it was his turn to seem more than a little uncomfortable. "I'll just finish my tea."

"Take your time," she replied, which was the exact opposite to the sentiment pounding in her heart. "There's... no rush."

Again the silence returned, and Julia was pretty sure that she wasn't the only one feeling awkward. She wasn't a great conversationalist at the best of times and her small talk game was lousy, but in that particular moment all she could think was that she really *needed* to get Piotr out of the house – albeit without arousing any suspicions. She was willing to let herself seem rude or brusque or downright unsociable if that was the price to pay for being left alone.

"Man, I should probably get going," he said finally, taking another sip of tea before setting the cup down still half full. "Thanks for the tea, but..."

"No problem."

"Yeah, I should..."

He hesitated, as if he thought he should come up with some other excuse, before mumbling something under his breath and heading to the back door.

"Thank God," Julia silently mouthed.

"As long as you haven't had any trouble with the ghost," he added, pulling the door open and turning to her. "You haven't seen or heard anything unusual here, have you?"

"Ghost?" she replied, furrowing her brow a little. "What ghost?"

CHAPTER FOURTEEN

"IT WAS YEARS AGO now," Piotr said, standing in the hallway and looking up at the loft hatch high above beyond the landing. "Before I was born. His name was Brian Gordon, he worked for my grandfather as a general all-round dogsbody and estate manager. This is the 1960s I think we're talking about."

Standing in the doorway that led back to the kitchen, Julia wasn't quite sure how she'd snatched defeat from the slathering jaws of victory. Piotr had been on his way out, only to take some unintended cue that made him think anyone cared about his little ghost story.

And she'd made the mistake of seeming interested.

"Anyway," he continued, "apparently it began to get out that old Brian had been fiddling the figures and pilfering from the estate for years. He'd always managed to cover it up, but my grandfather's sister – I think it was her – started to have suspicions. Eventually Brian realized that it was all going to come out, and he couldn't handle the shame. So supposedly one night he came out here to this house and he hung himself from that very hatch up there."

He kept his eyes fixed on the hatch, as if he was imagining the sight of the dead man.

"Ever since," he went on, "people have reported the odd strange sensation here at night. We don't mention it in the booking information and we tend not to spread it around, but I'm always interested to know whether anyone has seen or heard anything."

He turned to her.

"Well?"

"Well what?" she replied.

"It was your first night here last night," he continued. "Did you notice anything spooky?"

For a moment she thought back to the strange male figure on the landing.

"No," she said, slowly shaking her head. "Nothing."

"Huh. They said it's usually the first night he shows up, and then he either never appears again or – if he takes an interest in you – he might make his presence felt a few more times. He's supposedly harmless, but obviously anyone who sees a ghost, or thinks they see one, is going to get pretty scared. Am I right?"

"Probably," she said, wondering why he was even talking about such nonsense.

"Do you believe in ghosts?" he asked.

"Do I look like someone who believes in ghosts?" she replied.

"I don't know," he told her. "I don't know what someone would look like who -"

"I don't," she said firmly, before he could continue. "I never have and I never will. They're a stupid idea and anyone who believes in them needs their head testing."

"Right, so -"

"It's a childish superstition," she added. "I'd rather believe in fairies or unicorns. In the unlikely event that I *did* see some kind of ghostly figure, I'd just assume I was losing my mind. I definitely wouldn't start thinking that it was some dead person who'd come wandering back to haunt me."

"You seem pretty set on that."

"I don't have time for stupidity," she added, checking her watch yet again. "Actually, I don't have time for very much at the moment. I need to make lunch for Henry and myself, and then we've got a full day of activities planned, so if you don't mind..."

She let her voice trail off deliberately,

hoping that he might finally get the hint as the video game continued to let out a series of bangs and explosions in the front room.

"Of course," he said uneasily. "I'm sorry, the last thing you want is to have me standing here, nattering away about ghosts. Please, ignore everything I said to you and just get on with your holiday."

"That's what we're trying to do," she replied, forcing herself to be a little more firm this time. "I don't mean to be rude, but we're only here for the weekend and I'd really like to make the most of our time."

"I'll see myself out," he told her as he headed to the front door. "Like I said, I didn't mean to get in the way of your fun."

He glanced into the front room and spotted Henry on the sofa with the video game controller. At that moment the boy looked at him, and for a few seconds they watched each other as Henry opened his mouth and seemed poised to say something. Piotr waited, feeling more and more troubled by some niggling concern he couldn't quite place, and then he heard Julia clearing her throat.

Turning to her, he realized that she was clearly waiting for him to leave.

"Have a great rest of your time here," he said finally. "No need to call again, not unless you have any problems. On Monday morning just put the keys back in the box by the door and then I'll be by later to do the laundry and all that stuff. I hope you guys have a lot of fun."

"Don't worry," Julia said as more explosions rang out from the video game. "We will."

CHAPTER FIFTEEN

"OKAY, SO LET'S JUST get this on you," Julia said as she finished pulling the coat onto Henry. "It just about fits. I think it should do fine."

"It smells weird," he said, scrunching his nose up.

"It's perfectly clean," she told him, stepping back to make sure that he didn't look too strange. "I got it from a charity shop, but they wash everything before it's put out for sale. Or they steam it, at least."

Clearly not convinced, Henry looked down at the coat before taking a moment to sniff it again.

"It smells like mothballs," he pointed out.

"Well, it's better to have it than not to have it," she told him, trying to hide a sense of irritation. "We're going to go out and... take a little walk. We can't spend all day cooped up in here. You'll end up with square eyes if you play that video game all the time."

Turning, she made her way across the kitchen and grabbed her bag. She looked inside and saw her phone. Slipping it out, she double checked that it was still off before sliding it back in and closing the bag, and then she looked over her shoulder to see that Henry seemingly hadn't moved a muscle.

"Are you going to take me home on Monday?" he asked.

"What?"

"I just wondered," he continued, looking over at the window. "What's out there in the forest?"

"Nothing," she told him, puzzled by the question. "Trees. Probably some squirrels, stuff like that. There might even be deer. It stretches off for miles and miles in every direction, there's not even so much as another house anywhere nearby. Why?"

She waited for him to answer, but after a few seconds she began to realize why he was so scared. She wanted to tell him to stop being silly, to just trust her, but part of her worried that any such entreaties would only sound hollow and might even scare him more. She figured she needed to find a way to let him know that he was in no danger, without sounding like she was about to take him out and throw him into a shallow grave.

"I swear I'm not going to hurt you," she

realized, would sound pretty menacing given the circumstances.

"It's just a walk," she said finally. "It's just two people going for a walk, without any particular purpose in mind, and spending a few hours in the forest. Then we're going to come back and you can play on that game a little more, and by then it'll be dinner time and that'll be Saturday almost over."

Hoping that she might have calmed him down a little, she waited for a reply, yet once again he was merely staring back at her.

"That's normal," she continued. "It's just what normal people do. Don't your family ever take you out to do stuff like that?"

He slowly shook his head.

"Well, they should have," she told him. "If they had, maybe you and that Jake boy wouldn't have ended up -"

She caught herself just in time, and she had to pause for a few seconds while she waited for any little flare of anger to subside. She knew she could launch into a tirade, that she could really scream and cry, but she also knew that it would all be wasted energy – and she'd already wasted enough energy the day before at the service station. She didn't really have to much extra to spare. For days now she'd felt as if she was running on empty, and she felt pretty sure that – when everything came to an end on Monday – she was going to collapse and probably never get up again.

"It's going to be fun," she said firmly, sounding more like she was instructing him than offering encouragement. "You're going to have a good time."

CHAPTER SIXTEEN

TRAMPLING THROUGH THE FOREST, Henry picked his way between two more trees before stopping and looking over his shoulder.

"It's okay," Julia said, still several paces behind. "Keep going."

"In a straight line?" he asked nervously.

"Yeah, if you like," she continued, taking a moment to step over some brambles. "You can pick the route."

"But are we... going somewhere specific?"

"No, we're not going somewhere specific," she said with a sigh as she caught up to him. "Henry, please, just enjoy the walk, okay? It's supposed to be relaxing."

He continued to stare up at her.

"For both of us."

"You said we weren't going to go far from the house," he reminded her. "You said you wanted us to always be able to see it."

"Yes, well, I... changed my mind," she explained. "I thought we could go a bit further."

"Why don't you have a phone?" he asked.

"What?"

"You never look at your phone," he continued. "My mum and dad are always on their phones, all day, it's the only thing they ever like to look at. They get angry if anything distracts them from it. And then, the only time they *do* look away from it is when there's something on the TV that they want to watch, and even then they always have their phones with them. But you don't ever look at a phone. You don't even call anyone on it. Why not?"

"I... don't want to," she said, shocked by the question – and by the fact that he was so observant.

"Why not?"

"I just don't," she continued. "Not everyone's addicted to those things."

She glanced up at the sky for a moment before looking at him again.

"Not everyone wants to be contactable all the time or in touch with the world all the time or... tracked."

"I don't think it's a bad thing," Henry replied. "It makes it easier to talk to you. You seem like a nice person."

"A nice person?"

Staring at him for a moment, she wondered

whether he'd still say that if he knew what she was really thinking. She'd only come close to letting that show once, back at the service station when all her anger and rage had briefly burst out, but even then she'd managed to keep the absolute worst under wraps. He probably thought he'd seen it all, but for a few seconds she wondered how he'd react if she told him what she actually thought of him.

If she told him how much she *hated* him for what he'd done.

"I want to kill them," she remembered telling her friend Jackie a few days earlier. "I want to find them both and I want to kill them, and I want to make them suffer the same way -"

"No, you really don't," Jackie had told her, with tears streaming down her face. "Julia, you're not that kind of person. I know you're not. You're just hurting, that's all. I can't even begin to imagine what you're going through right now."

"Maybe I've changed," she'd snarled through gritted teeth, and she'd really believed those words too. "Don't I have the right? I think I have *every* right. No-one would blame me if I found those boys and I made them feel the same pain that -"

"You'd blame yourself!" Jackie had hissed, grabbing her by the sides of her arms as if to hold her in place. "You're not going to let this turn you into a monster, Julia. I will never let that happen!"

"That's easy for you to say," she'd replied.

"Not just me," Jackie had said firmly. "Come on, Julia, you know this isn't the right way to think. Do you really think Ben would want you to do anything bad?"

As those words echoed in her mind, Julia realized that she'd begun to drift away into her memories. At the same time, she also felt a solitary tear in one corner of her eye; before she could react, the tear began to run down her cheek. Just allowing herself to hear Ben's name – even only in her thoughts, in her memories – had threatened to pull down the dam she'd built in her head. For a few seconds she worried that she might not be able to force everything back under control, but finally – after clenching her fists for a moment – she felt a sense of calm returning.

In her mind's eye, she briefly imagined a grave in the forest, and she knew she could do anything she wanted and no-one would be able to stop her in time. Still, she managed to force that idea far from her thoughts as she reminded herself that she simply needed to stick to the plan and avoid another meltdown.

Taking a deep breath, she realized that once again the storm had passed.

"Sorry," she murmured, not quite sure how long she'd spent in silence. "I just -"

And then, before she could finish, she

realized that Henry was gone. She turned and looked all around, convinced that he must have just gone to look at something, but instead she saw no sign of him at all. As a sense of horror and panic began to swell in her chest, she turned around again but she understood now that her brief dazed moment had allowed him to get away.

"Henry!" she screamed, terrified by the thought that he could have run off in any direction. "Where are you? Henry, get back here!"

CHAPTER SEVENTEEN

RACING THROUGH THE FOREST, almost tripping with every step, Henry could hear his own ragged breaths above the sound of his feet crashing through the dead leaves.

A moment later, convinced that he was about to be caught, he looked over his shoulder. He saw no sign of Julia, but then – just as he turned to look ahead again – he slammed into a tree and let out a pained gasp as he tumbled own and hit the ground, quickly rolling down the slope before bumping against another tree and finally coming to a stop.

Panicking, he sat up and leaned against the tree as he looked back the way he'd just come, but after a few seconds he realized to his immense relief that he was alone.

He was free.

At first he hadn't quite dared to believe he had a chance. Julia had fallen silent and had seemed to be in a complete daze – much like the daze at the service station – but this time he'd acted faster; this time he'd turned immediately and had started running, and he'd been amazed that she hadn't reacted at all. He'd kept running for several more minutes, but now as he remained sitting on the forest floor he realized that he had no idea which way to go. He didn't even know which way was north.

Hauling himself up, he brushed dead leaves from the coat he'd been given as he looked around and hoped to spot some kind of clue. His heart was pounding and all he could think was that he had to get home, and that he couldn't let Julia catch him again. As much as she'd tried to insist that she wasn't going to hurt him, he felt that there couldn't be any other reason why she would have kidnapped him in the first place.

"I only want to talk to you," he remembered her saying a day earlier, when she'd first grabbed him. "You know who I am, don't you? You're not safe here. I don't know if you know what happened to your friend Jake, but I have to make sure it doesn't happen to you too. And there's only one way to do that."

He'd struggled at first, but he hadn't managed to stop her. Then she'd talked to him some more and she'd sort of explained at least part of it and he'd realized that he needed to go along with her, at least for a while.

But now...

Now, standing all alone in the forest, he knew that this might be his last chance to get away, but he also knew that she was close somewhere and that if he took the wrong turn, she'd find him again and this time she'd be angrier than ever. This time, she might use some of the stuff he'd seen in the boot of her car.

Sniffing back tears, he began to pick his way down the slope, reaching out carefully to steady himself against the trees. More than anything in the world, he wanted his mum and dad to suddenly appear and lead him to safety; he knew they'd been angry at him recently, to the point that they'd barely been able to look him in the eye, but he still believed that they were going to show up and save him.

He just had to find them, wherever they were in the vast forest. Because he knew one thing with absolute certainty: they had to be looking for him.

CHAPTER EIGHTEEN

"POLICE HAVE ASKED THAT anyone with information should call the number immediately," the reporter continued, "and that under no circumstances should Mrs. Parker be approached."

As the video ended, Piotr tapped the screen and leaned back in his seat. Having parked his S.U.V. a short distance from the house, he'd spent some time investigating a few theories, but so far he hadn't quite managed to come up with any conclusive proof to back up his suspicions.

Still...

Bringing up the photo of Julia Parker again, he couldn't help but feel that – despite the significant differences in their hair, make-up, clothing and just about every facet of their appearance – this was the Julia *Jenkins* he'd met at the house. He'd double-checked the booking information and Jenkins was definitely the information he'd been given, and he assumed that the booking site itself handled identification issues, but now he was starting to wonder whether a smart and motivated person might be able to fake some of their details.

That might also, he realized now, be why this particular booking had arrived via one of the lesser known sites.

Then there was the kid. He scrolled up the page until he saw a photo of police cars parked outside a primary school. There were no images of either Jacob Handley or Henry Dartmore, since their identities were clearly being protected even though their names had leaked online, but the Henry kid in the house had certainly been in the right age bracket and – crucially – something about the boy had just seemed very 'off', as if he'd been terrified.

As much as he didn't want to start coming up with crazy theories, in that moment Piotr found himself piecing together the various fragmentary clues and trying to work out whether he'd stumbled upon something pretty huge.

"Fuck it," he said finally, unbuckling his seat belt and climbing out of the car, then slamming the door shut and looking back along the road.

He was about fifteen minutes from the house, assuming he returned on foot, and he figured that he could easily approach through the forest. He was more than accustomed to sneaking up on game birds, so he assumed that he'd have a good chance of getting all the way to the house without attracting attention. Although he had no intention of actually confronting the woman, part of him felt that he needed a little more information before he could even think about calling the police.

Something about Julia 'Jenkins' (if that was even her real surname) just felt extremely wrong.

He took a moment to reconsider his options, and then he checked his phone before starting to walk back along the road. As he did so, he pulled up some more information about the grisly case; he'd heard plenty about it over the weeks, of course, and like pretty much everyone in the country he'd been utterly horrified as more details had emerged every single day.

How could such evil exist in the world?

How could such evil exist in children?

To be honest, he'd tried to avoid asking himself those questions too deeply? With two kids of his own – a girl aged five and a boy aged three – he'd simply tried to focus on the fact that he and his wife were raising their children properly, and that Emily and Harrison would never in a million years do something so awful. Nevertheless, in the back of his mind he couldn't help but wonder whether evil had some insidious way of creeping into places where it should never belong, whether it could blossom in a person's heart and soul even without a seed.

Even without being nurtured.

Especially without being nurtured.

As he stepped off the road and continued his journey on rougher ground, he continued to remind himself of the details. After adjusting his earbuds, he tapped to play another video.

"Eight-year-old Benjamin Parker died three weeks ago," another reporter explained, "after being led away from the school playground by two older boys from another class. Yesterday news broke that one of the young suspects had died following an unexplained incident at a home in Lancaster. Further news yesterday, that the other suspect has disappeared, has been met with condemnation from politicians in all parties, who are asking whether the police have handled the case appropriately."

He clicked back and then brought up another video.

"We all know what's going on here," some random vlogger was saying angrily, with evident agitation in his voice. "The mainstream media won't report it, they hide behind all these so-called rules, but the truth is all over the net. Julia Parker has kidnapped one of the kids who murdered her son Ben, and that's shortly after the other murderer was killed. Now, we don't know exactly what happened to Jacob and how he died, but does anyone really believe that these are all coincidences? I mean, if you do, I've got a bridge you might be interested in. But let's face facts. Julia Parker allegedly killed Jacob Handley and now she's kidnapped Henry Dartmore. It's not hard to see where this is all headed."

Feeling a branch cracking under his right foot, Piotr froze. Realizing that he needed to be far more cautious, he slipping his phone away and took his earbuds out. He could see the house in the distance, beyond the farthest trees, and he told himself that he just had to sneak a little closer and make sure that he was right about what was happening. And then he could call the police and get them to deal with the whole situation, because the absolute last thing he wanted was to get involved in some kind of national news story.

He just wanted a quiet life with a minimal amount of fuss and bother. More than anything, he just wanted to be left alone.

CHAPTER NINETEEN

FINALLY DARING TO TAKE another step forward, Henry immediately froze as a twig snapped beneath his left foot. He stayed completely motionless for a few seconds, terrified that he might have given up his location, and then he looked around and saw that there was still no sign of Julia.

After holding his breath for a moment, he stepped forward again.

The ground had leveled out a little but he still saw nothing but trees in every direction. Julia had mentioned that the house was miles and miles from anywhere and he was starting to realize that she'd been telling the truth, although he supposed that eventually he *had* to reach civilization. He could see the sun above, almost breaking through a thick covering of clouds, but he wasn't quite sure how to use that fact to work out which way was north.

And even if he found north, he had no idea whether he should go in that direction.

A moment later he heard a very faint and distant humming sound. He watched the sky, and sure enough a small plane appeared.

Although he knew he was probably too far away to be seen, Henry began to wave his arms furiously. For the next couple of minutes he did everything in his power to attract attention – everything apart from shouting, that is – but gradually the plane moved further away until finally it was gone.

Lowering his arms, he told himself that there was still a chance they might have spotted him, and that they might already be radioing for help.

Feeling a little warm, he began to slip out of the coat Julia had given him. He still hated the smell of the damn thing, and he dropped it onto the ground as he began to walk again. He knew that an adult would probably be much better at getting to safety, but he'd grown up in a town and he'd never had to try surviving out in the middle of nowhere. He was fairly sure that there weren't wolves or other dangerous creatures in Britain, but he couldn't help looking around every few minutes just in case something ravenous and hideous might show up.

A moment later, hearing another twig

snapping, he stopped in his tracks.

Turning, he looked back the way he'd just come. He saw the coat on the ground and wondered whether he should go back and get it, but he told himself that there was no point wasting time. As for the twig snapping, he figured that could have been caused by anything, although for a few seconds he couldn't help imagining something fierce – like a wolf, perhaps, or even an escaped lion or tiger from a zoo – suddenly stepping into view with thick saliva drooling as it opened its mouth to reveal huge fangs.

Taking a deep breath, he tried to remind himself that animals didn't escape from zoos often, and that there was no reason to worry that one might be around now.

He turned to -

"What the hell are you doing?" Julia snapped angrily, appearing as if from nowhere and grabbing him by the arm, then twisting him round and slamming him against the nearest tree. "Have you completely lost your mind?"

Although his first instinct was to try to pull away, Henry immediately felt that her grip on his arm was too tight.

"Do you still not get it?" she continued as he tried to wriggle free. "Do you think I just brought you out here for fun?"

"Let me -"

"I'm trying to save your life!" she shouted, pinning him against the tree and holding him in place as she dropped to her knees and looked into his eyes. "Can't you get that through your thick little head? No-one else understands what's happening here but I'm trying to keep you alive!"

"I want to go home," he sobbed, unable to stop the waterworks as tears flooded from his eyes.

"Do you think anyone *wants* you at home?" she snarled. "Do you think they want to see your face again?"

"I -"

"Because they don't!" she sneered. "They hate you, like everyone hates you!"

"No, I -"

"Even *I* hate you," she continued breathlessly, glaring at him as her eyes filled with cool white anger. "Everyone in the world hates you but I'm still trying to help you, you little piece of -"

Stopping herself just in time, she realized that he was breaking down, that he was shaking with sorrow as he cried frantically. Her first instinct was to scream at him to stop, but she knew that wouldn't work. Instead she glanced around to make sure that no-one – and nothing – had spotted them, and then she turned to him again and tried to logically work out how best to get him on her side.

Looking up at the sky, she saw no sign of the plane. She'd spotted it too, a few minutes earlier, and part of her worried that it was some kind of police operation. She quickly reminded herself, however, that she'd covered her tracks well.

"I'm trying to help you," she said for what she knew must be the twentieth time as she turned to Henry again. "Just try to understand that, okay? I'm trying to help and... and frankly I'm probably the only person in the world who *can* help you right now. Because I'm probably the only person who understands what happened to your little friend, and what'll happen to you if..."

Her voice trailed off.

She looked around again, still terrified that she might spot something.

"You just need to trust me," she continued finally, turning back to him. "You've got no choice, it's either trust me or... or something really bad'll happen to you. You heard about your friend Jacob, right? Do you want the same thing to happen to you?"

"What happened to Jake?" he whimpered.

"You don't want to know," she told him, sidestepping the fact that she wasn't quite sure about the details either – but that she certainly had her suspicions. "Your only chance is to stick with me for a few days. Because if I'm right, I'm the only person who has any chance of saving your miserable little life. Do you get it now?"

CHAPTER TWENTY

AS CAREFULLY AS HE turned the door handle, Piotr couldn't help but make a noise. The handle creaked ever so slightly, but he figured that was okay as he slowly opened the back door and looked into the house's kitchen.

So far, so good.

He knew Julia the boy were still out, and he figured that nobody would just go for just a short walk in such a large forest, so he figured that he had plenty of time. Half an hour, at least. So after looking over his shoulder once more to triple check that he wasn't being watched, he pushed the door all the way open and stepped inside.

In truth, he wasn't sure what he expected to find. As he stepped across the kitchen, he certainly saw no sign of a miraculously convenient confession anywhere, or a pile of newspaper cuttings that might confirm his suspicions. Instead he could only note that the place seemed strangely untouched, as if Julia had barely begun to make herself comfortable. There was something about the woman that seemed extremely highly strung, but after a moment he spotted a handbag on the counter and he realized that he might be lucky after all.

After checking that there was no sign of anyone in the hallway, he hurried to the bag and pulled it open.

Reaching inside, he immediately found the purse and pulled it out. His hands were trembling slightly as he opened it up, and then he froze as soon as he saw the woman's driving license.

Julia Parker.

Okay.

So he was right.

It was her.

"Fucking hell," he mouthed almost silently, trying to stay calm. "What kind of sick -"

Before he could finish, he heard a bumping sound. Looking up at the ceiling, he tried to stay calm as silence returned to the house. He'd spent enough time there over the years to know that the place had an awful habit of emitting these strange and seemingly random sounds, and he also very much believed the ghost story he'd mentioned to Julia earlier. He'd never actually seen anything himself, but he had little doubt that the ghost of old

Brian Gordon might well be floating around.

"Give me a break, Brian," he said softly. "We're on the same side here."

He waited, but now he heard only silence.

"That's better," he added. "You can go back to haunting the place or whatever it is that counts as fun for a ghost. I'll deal with the whole kidnapped kid situation."

And then, turning to look out into the hallway, he realized that he could hear footsteps in the distance.

Setting the purse back into the handbag, he headed to the window and peered out, and to his horror he saw that Julia and the boy were already making their way back.

Looking around, he tried to figure out how he was going to get away, and finally he hurried to the back door. As soon as he was outside he gently bumped the door shut, and he told himself that he could simply sprint away back into the forest as soon as he heard the front door opening. The last thing he wanted was any kind of confrontation.

After all, he'd seen enough proof.

He could call the police now.

He waited, trying to stay calm, and finally he heard the telltale sound of the house's front door opening. Figuring that this was his only chance, he turned and hurried along the side of the house, ready to make a break for the trees. With any luck, he told himself, he could get away without even being seen; and even if he *was* spotted, well, would that really matter? After all, what if -

Suddenly Julia stepped in front of him so abruptly that he almost slammed straight into her.

"Hey," she said, staring at him with a furrowed brow.

"Hey," he stammered, taking a step back.

"I thought you left," she told him.

"I did," he replied, and now his mind was racing as he desperately tried to think of an excuse. "I just came back to... see if you had enough wood."

"Oh."

"Yeah," he replied, turning and looking over at the wood piled up in a small shelter near the back door. "But it looks like you do, so I suppose that's fine."

He took a deep breath, trying very hard to seem as if he wasn't giving the matter too much thought while also trying not to act like he was desperate to get away.

"But you've got plenty," he added, turning to her again, "so -"

Before he could finish, Julia slammed the shovel against the side of his head, knocking him out instantly and sending his body crumpling down against the dead leaves.

CHAPTER TWENTY-ONE

AS HE CONTINUED TO play the video game, Henry couldn't help but glance at the window. He'd been playing for hours now, and although normally he'd have loved nothing more than a day spent doing nothing much at all, this time he couldn't shake the feeling that he didn't really have any other choice.

The sun was starting to set outside. A moment later he heard the car boot slamming shut. Julia had been hurrying in and out of the house for a while now, sometimes going down into the basement long periods of time, but a moment later he heard her stepping back inside and this time she sounded less frantic.

Finally she made her way into the doorway.

"Hey there," she said slightly breathlessly.

He forced a smile, but he knew it wasn't

very convincing.

"Is everything okay in here?" she asked.

He nodded.

"How are you doing with the game?"

"Okay."

"Only okay? I thought you'd be an expert by now."

He knew she was making small talk, that she was trying to act like everything was fine, but he couldn't quite bring himself to join in. Something was different, too; ever since they'd returned from their ill-fated walk in the forest, she'd seemed much more nervous and he'd even heard her sometimes talking to herself under her breath. She'd also been bringing a *lot* of stuff in from the car and taking it straight down into the basement.

"Are you hungry?" she asked.

He shrugged.

"It's a little early still," she continued, checking her watch, "but I suppose I could make a start with the -"

Suddenly a loud rumble filled the air, lasting for several seconds before subsiding.

Henry turned and looked at the window, just in time to see that the panes of glass were shaking slightly.

"There might be some bad weather on the way," Julia told him. "It wasn't on the forecast yesterday but it's there now. There's a storm coming in, it should just miss us but there's a chance we'll get the tail of it. You're not scared of storms, are you?"

He thought for a moment, and then he shook his head.

"I'll go and do a few things in the kitchen," she replied, turning to walk away. "Just keep playing for a while, okay?"

"Are you?"

She stopped and looked back at him, and for a moment she seemed utterly confused.

"Am I what?" she said cautiously.

"Scared of storms."

"Of course not," she told him, although he wasn't sure that he entirely believed her. "There's nothing to be scared *of.* It's just some bad weather, that's all. It'll pass."

CHAPTER TWENTY-TWO

RAIN BEGAN TO SPIT at the window. Not a lot, but enough to promise that there was a lot more to come as the evening darkened and a flash of lightning briefly filled the gloomy sky.

A few seconds later the thunder returned, rumbling low and long as the panes rattled once more.

Sitting at the kitchen table, Julia continued to stare down at the photo she was holding in her left hand, while her right hand absent-mindedly twiddled with the necklace she was wearing. Her eyes were filled with tears, none of which had escaped yet and run down her cheeks, but she'd been sitting in silence for several minutes now and she couldn't bring herself to look away from the photo.

The image showed a young boy, slightly

younger than Henry, smiling at the camera while holding a toy police car in one hand. Julia remembered exactly where and when she'd bought that police car for him: she'd been visiting a friend in one of the villages and she'd popped into a local shop, and for some reason the little car had caught her eye. She'd dithered briefly, not wanting to buy her son too many things, but finally she'd broken down and picked it up for him. Then she'd waited a couple of weeks and given it to him after he got a perfect score in a school spelling test, and he'd been so pleased with it and...

That had been about six months earlier.

"You spoil him," Al had said, half jokingly and half serious.

"I don't," she'd replied.

"I'm not saying it's necessarily a bad thing," he'd continued. "I'm just not sure how I'm going to keep up. You're going to turn him into a real mummy's boy."

Now, as she sat in silence at the table and stared into the photo, she felt one single tear running from her eye and tracking down her cheek. She waited until it was almost at her lips before reaching up and wiping it away.

"Julia?"

Startled, she turned to see that Henry was standing in the doorway. Immediately realizing that he could see the photo, she turned it around and shoved it into her pocket.

"What?" she asked quickly.

She waited, but she could tell that the sight of that particular photo had shocked the boy.

"What?" she asked again, keen to change the subject. "Are you done with the game?"

"Was that a picture of -"

"What do you want?" she snapped.

He paused, as if he was too scared to continue.

"What is it?" she asked, trying to seem more friendly. "Did something scare you?"

"I heard something."

"What did you hear?"

"I don't know," he said cautiously, "but..."

He hesitated, and then he slowly turned and looked toward the bottom of the staircase.

"You didn't hear anything," she told him, just as thunder rumbled again. In the space of just a few minutes, the rain outside had already become more intense. "It's just the storm."

She watched him, but he was still staring at the staircase.

Sighing, she got to her feet and walked over to join him.

"It's going to be quite a strong storm," she continued, hoping to calm him down. "I checked the weather forecast on the television and the weather's really taking a turn for the worse. It's probably going to make the house make a lot of noises. If we start worrying about every little one of those noises, we'll end up... well, I think we might both lose our minds."

A moment later, as if to emphasize that point, a groaning sound briefly rang out from somewhere high up, as if the wind had managed to somehow penetrate the rafters.

"Hear that?" she asked. "You've obviously got a strong imagination and I'm sure you think maybe it's a ghost, but it's not. It's caused by a small hole somewhere that's allowing the wind inside, and if the storm gets worse then the sounds are going to get louder as well. Do you understand now?"

Looking down at him, she saw the fear in his eyes.

"Henry? Do you understand?"

He hesitated, and then he slowly nodded.

"We're both going to have to be brave," she added with a smile, reaching out and putting a (hopefully) reassuring hand on his shoulder. "I'm sure you can do it, though. Just remember that the storm is out there and we're safe and snug in here, and we just have to ride it out until the morning. I checked the forecast yesterday and there really wasn't anything about a storm before, but obviously it's coming in now. But by the morning it'll all be over. At least we don't live in America where they get all those awful hurricanes. Can you imagine that?"

"I'd like to see a hurricane," he replied.

"I bet you would," she said with a faint chuckle, as the lights briefly flickered. "Listen, go and play on your game while we've still got power, because in a place like this you never know when there might be a cut. And I'm going to search out some more candles."

"Do you really think there'll be a power cut?" he asked, clearly scared by the idea.

"There might be," she replied, before leaning down and kissing the top of his head. "Sweetheart, if -"

Suddenly she froze, horrified by what she'd just done. Pulling back, she saw the same expression of shock in Henry's eyes; for a moment, for just a fraction of a second, some other instinct had kicked in and she'd almost forgotten that she wasn't talking to her own son. She wanted to explain, to tell him that it meant nothing, but she couldn't quite get those words out of her mouth. Instead she realized that her own maternal instincts had briefly countered everything else, and she wanted to scream and punch a hole in the wall.

"Go back in there," she stammered, nodding toward the front room.

"But -"

"Go back in there!" she shouted angrily, grabbing his arm and shoving him through the open doorway with such force that – as she let go – he tripped on a slightly loose board and fell, landing hard on his knees. "Just stay in there," she continued, no longer able to hide a sense of fury. "And... and don't come out until I tell you that dinner's ready, okay?"

Stumbling to his feet, he seemed frozen for a moment before finally heading back over to the sofa.

"I mean it," she continued, filled with a growing sense of panic as she tried to pull her raging fears back under control. "Don't make me have to start checking up on you, Henry. That'd only make me angry and, well, I don't think you want me to be angry. Not tonight. So just do as you're told, okay?"

He nodded.

After stepping back through to the kitchen, Julia took a moment to lean against the wall. Until that moment she'd managed to somehow keep her anger mostly under control, but now she was furious at herself for momentarily breaking. She couldn't help wondering what had possessed her, and after a few seconds she began to sob frantically as she slid down until she was sitting on the floor. The video game was playing loudly in the front room and rain was tapping more heavily at the windows as she put her hands over her face and broke into a series of huge, shuddering sobs.

"I'm sorry," she spluttered, overcome by guilt. "Ben, I'm so sorry. Please, you have to forgive me."

CHAPTER TWENTY-THREE

AS HIS EYES SLOWLY slid open, Piotr noticed an overwhelming stench of dirt and damp and mold. He blinked a couple of times in the darkness, and a few more seconds passed before he realized that he was on his side on the floor, and that his hands were tied behind his back.

Immediately trying to sit up, he found that not only were plastic tags tied tight around his wrists, but more had been pulled even tighter around his ankles. He struggled a couple of times, trying to force them loose, before rolling onto his back and looking up to see several pipes running across the ceiling. There was just enough light breaking through a dirty little window at the top of the far wall to allow him to see thick cobwebs hanging from those pipes, and a moment later he looked to his right and saw a set of rickety old shelves holding half a dozen paint cans.

Finally he realized where he was.

The basement.

"I just came back to... see if you had enough wood," he remembered telling Julia.

"Oh."

"Yeah," he'd continued, even as he'd rapidly begun to realize that his excuse was threadbare and obvious. "But it looks like you do, so I suppose that's fine."

He'd hesitated, hoping that she was simply going to let the matter rest.

"But you've got plenty," he'd added, turning to her again, "so -"

And then she'd hit him. He wasn't even sure that he remembered quite *what* she'd used, but he'd seen the shock in her eyes as she'd swung something against his head. He wasn't sure how long ago that had been, but as he looked up at the window he saw that the sky was much darker now and he heard rain lashing against the glass. A few seconds after that he saw a flash of lightning followed swiftly by a peal of thunder and he furrowed his brow.

He'd checked the weather app that morning, just as he checked it *every* morning, and he was sure that there'd been no mention of any storm.

Figuring that he could worry about that later, he began to pull on the plastic ties around his wrists. If he could get those loose, he told himself, then he could deal with everything else. There was no gag over his mouth, but he knew why: there was no point yelling, and making any kind of noise would most likely just attract Julia's attention. Far better, he supposed, to pretend to be still unconscious so that he could work in peace, although so far he could tell that he wasn't having much luck with the ties.

"Come on," he muttered under his breath, "you can -"

Before he was able to finish, he heard footsteps above. Looking up at the pipes again, he listened as someone walked across the floor above the basement, and he quickly realized that he was more or less directly beneath the kitchen. Julia was up there and in that moment he began to wonder exactly what she intended to do with him. Sure, she hadn't killed him so far, but what if she was just working up to that moment?

She might not be a cold-blooded killer, but she was a grieving mother who'd clearly lost her mind. He knew that people could become very dangerous if they were cornered.

Realizing that he had to find a way to get free, he pulled on the plastic ties for a moment longer before stopping and looking around. He felt sure that there had to be something in the basement he could use, something he could rub against the

ties in an attempt to get them to split open.
And he knew he had to work fast.

CHAPTER TWENTY-FOUR

"SO THIS IS, UM..."

As those words left her mouth, Julia stood in front of the cooker and stared into the pot of ready-made bolognese, and for a few seconds she couldn't even remember what she'd been heating up. Her mind was racing and she could only think about the guy tied up in the basement, and she had to really force herself to focus on the task at hand.

"Uh, it's bolognese," she said finally, before looking at the second pot, in which spaghetti was boiling away. "It's spaghetti bolognese. You like that, don't you?"

Turning, she saw that Henry was watching her from the doorway and that – if anything – there was now even *more* fear in his eyes.

"Who doesn't like spaghetti bolognese?" she continued, forcing yet another weak smile.

"Everyone likes it, it's like almost a new national dish in this country after Sunday roasts and fish and chips. It was always Ben's -"

Stopping herself just in time, she realized that she really didn't need to bring his name up.

"Sit down," she added.

Henry obediently headed to the table and sat on one of the chairs, as if he was too scared to disobey an order. As he did so, a particularly strong gust of wind hit the house and caused the walls to creak, but this time the boy knew better than to show any obvious fear.

"That's better," Julia said, determined to maintain at least an illusion of normality.

Turning to the pots again, she grabbed one of the spoons and began to stir the spaghetti.

"Not too long now," she continued, "and -"

Suddenly a loud splitting sound filled the air. Startled, she turned around so fast that she dropped the spoon and sent it clattering against the floor. As the sound faded, she looked over at the empty doorway at the exact moment that the lights flickered again, and it took a few more seconds before she was able to pull herself together again.

"That was nothing," she stammered, trying in vain to sound as if she wasn't scared at all. "It was just the wind hitting the house. You realize that, don't you?"

She turned to Henry.

He nodded quickly – again, as if he was too scared to cross her.

"See what I mean?" she said, trying to act natural now as she picked the spoon up and began to rinse it under the tap. "You're not the only one who can get a little jittery when there's a storm. Even adults do. It's part of human nature, really. What you have to remember, though, is that we're safe and sound in here, and that the storm can't get to us. And it'll pass. Storms always do. That's why they're called storms and not just... weather."

She waited for a reply, but after a few seconds Henry turned and looked over at the opposite counter. Following his gaze, Julia wasn't sure at first what he was looking at – until she realized that she'd left out several of the plastic ties and ropes and other items she'd hurriedly fetched from the car earlier.

"Don't mind that stuff," she said, hurrying over and grabbing everything, then shoving it into the nearest drawer. "I was just sorting through it, that's all."

"I won't try to run away again," he told her.

"I know."

"You're not going to tie me up, are you?"

"Of course I'm not going to tie you up."

"But you said -"

"That was just an empty threat," she stammered, trying desperately to stay calm as she turned to him again. "Can we please both just forget about the service station?"

"But you said that I -"

"I know what I said!" she shouted angrily, before taking a moment to get her anger back under control. "I was panicking, that's all," she told him. "Can you just give me a break? I've made a nice meal for us both and it's nearly ready." She looked around, and in that moment she spotted the phone she'd pulled from Piotr's pockets while she was dragging him down into the basement and tying him up. "Wait here," she added, hurrying over and grabbing the phone, then heading to the door. "I mean it. If I hear any hint that you're leaving this room, I'll be mad. Really mad. And the doors are locked, and the windows too, so don't even think about trying anything."

As soon as she was in the hallway, she stopped and tried to unlock the phone. She was far from a master hacker, however, so after just a few seconds she realized that the situation was hopeless and that there was no way to magically bypass the need for a code. At the same time, she'd gone twenty-four hours now without much news of the outside world and although she couldn't risk turning on the television in case Henry overheard anything, there were several things that she really needed to check.

"Stay right where you are, okay?" she called

out to Henry again. "I'll be back in a couple of minutes. Just... don't move a muscle. Do you understand?"

"Yes," he replied softly, barely raising his voice above a whisper.

She hesitated, still wondering whether she might be about to make a big mistake, before heading over to the door that led down into the basement.

CHAPTER TWENTY-FIVE

CROUCHING DOWN, BARELY ABLE to see anything in the darkness, Julia used the light from the phone's screen to take hold of Piotr's hand and turn it around. She extended the thumb and pressed it against the screen, hoping against hope that this would somehow unlock it, yet nothing happened.

Sighing, she let go of his hand. And then, as she looked at his face, she saw that he wasn't unconscious at all. Instead, one eye was open and staring back at her. For a moment she wasn't sure how to react; she'd been so sure that he was out cold and now she realized that she was going to have to explain herself.

"I need your code," she stammered.

She waited, but he merely continued to watch her face. Although she'd told herself that she hadn't hit him *that* hard, part of her was starting to worry that she might have caused him some serious damage.

"I need your code," she continued, holding the phone up for him to see. "I'm not going to hurt you, I just... I need to check something."

"Let me go," he gasped.

"Not right now."

"People are going to be worried about me," he continued. "They're going to start looking for me."

"You work on an estate," she countered. "They're probably used to you being out late."

"Not *this* late," he replied, turning to her slightly, revealing the bloodied wound on one side of his forehead, causing by the impact with the shovel. "They're going to call the police. Do you really think they won't eventually find their way here?"

"I -"

"I know who you are," he continued.

"You don't know anything," she sneered through gritted teeth.

"You're the woman they're looking for," he pointed out. "The one whose... I know what happened to you. I know your son was murdered."

"Shut up!" she snapped.

"I know they arrested two of the other boys from his school. I know there are rumors that one of those boys died and that you kidnapped the other one. I can't even begin to understand what you're going through, but you can't think that revenge is the best option. Even if those two boys killed your son, that doesn't mean you can do the same thing to them."

"Is that really what you think is happening here?" she asked.

"Please just let me go," he replied, and now there were tears in his eyes. "I should never have come to check up on you. I'm sorry. But if you let me go, I won't tell a soul that I ever saw you."

"I need the code for your phone," she said again. "I need to know what's going on out there and I can't risk turning mine on in case they track it. Give me the code for your phone and then I'll... I'll see how things are going. Believe me, I don't want to hurt you. I don't want to hurt anyone. I just need to know what's going on."

She waited, and she was starting to hope that perhaps she was getting through to him.

"If I give you the code," he said cautiously, "will you let me go?"

"Your odds will be better," she replied. "Put it like that."

Again she waited.

"Eight," he said finally, "two, nine... four."

"The same as the box with the keys?"

He nodded.

Tapping that number onto the screen, she let out a sigh of relief as the phone revealed its main screen. Getting to her feet, she turned and hurried toward the steps.

"Hey!" he gasped. "You said you'd let me go!"

"I said I'd think about it," she replied, already hurrying up to the door. "I can't just let you wander off. I'll figure it all out eventually. Right now, you just have to stay down here."

"I have children of my own," he called after her. "I know it must hurt, everything that happened to you, but hurting other people won't make you feel any better. Hurting that boy up there, because of what he did to your own son, won't change anything!"

"I'm not an idiot," she said, stopping and looking back down at him for a moment. "And I'm not a killer, either. I didn't bring Henry out here to hurt him. I brought him out here to protect him."

"From who?"

"Just stay down here," she added, more firmly than before. "When the time is right, I *will* let you go. I promise."

CHAPTER TWENTY-SIX

THE WATER IN THE pasta pot was bubbling fast as Julia hurried over and grabbed the spoon. Still holding the phone in one hand, she used the other to stir the spaghetti before lifting some out, only to find that the strands were too soggy now to hold together.

"Damn it," she muttered under her breath, before looking into the pan and seeing that the meat and the sauce were starting to burn. "Idiot."

She moved both pots away from the heat and turned the stove off, and then she looked at the phone again. Even in just the short time it had taken her to hurry up from the basement, she'd managed to bring up a news story about Henry's disappearance, but so far the police didn't really seem to have too many leads. Then again, as she scrolled down the page, she realized that they might not necessarily announce everything that they knew.

Sometimes she worried that she was giving the police too much credit, and that they weren't deploying state of the art high-tech devices to track her down. At other times, however, she felt sure that they had plenty of tricks up their sleeves and that it was a miracle she'd managed to evade capture for so long. Any second now there could be a knock at the door, or perhaps the door would simply be smashed out of the way as a swarm of officers flooded into the house. She imagined herself being thrown down against the floor with a gun aimed at the back of her head while voices shouted all around.

And then, scrolling further down the page, she saw him.

A video was ready to play, and she could already see an image of her husband sitting flanked by two police officers. She had no doubt that this was some desperate attempt to get her to turn herself in, but she felt a frisson of anger as she reminded herself that they had no idea what was really happening. Even Al felt like an enemy in that moment, and she couldn't ignore a flicker of disgust as it ran through her bones.

"You don't understand," she whispered under her breath as she looked at the slightly grainy image of her husband's face. "You never got it."

Somehow, ever since Ben had died, she'd felt completely alone. She knew she was being cruel to Al, that he needed her support, yet he'd been so placid throughout the ordeal – as if he had no intention of trying to fight back. He'd just accepted everything, and in the end she hadn't even bothered to tell him about her worst fears or about her plan to save Henry.

"You'd have tried to stop me," she murmured. "I know it. You -"

Suddenly realizing that she was talking to herself, she turned and saw Henry sitting patiently at the table – and in that moment she felt a rush of relief at the thought that this time he'd obeyed her commands.

"Dinner's... nearby ready," she stammered, before tapping to go back to the main news page. "It's not -"

Suddenly she froze as she saw another headline, this time warning about possible disruption in the country due to the oncoming storm. She tapped to read the story, and already a sense of dread was starting to spread through her bones.

"Meteorologists continue to insist that there were no signs of the storm developing as recently as twelve hours ago," she whispered as she read out loud from the page, "but experts say that this doesn't necessarily mean that warnings were missed. Instead, Storm -"

Stopping, she had to read the next line a

couple of times before it sank in properly.

"Instead, Storm Ben is believed to be a rare but not unprecedented example of a major storm front developing in conditions where..."

Her voice trailed off.

"Storm Ben," she said again, and now her voice was trembling with fear. "Why does it have to be called Storm Ben?"

She scrolled down the page, scanning the text and finally finding mention of the fact that this was the second named storm of the season. Storm Alexis had hit about three weeks earlier, and she had some vague memory that storms were always named in alphabetical order; still, as much as she tried to convince herself that the whole thing was a massive coincidence, she couldn't help but feel struck by the fact that this Storm Ben phenomenon seemed to have developed very quickly and that – based on the images further down the page – it appeared to be bearing down almost directly onto her position.

"It's just a coincidence," she said, turning to Henry. "You get that, right? It's all just one big coincidence."

She waited for a reply, but she already knew that he had no idea what she was talking about. A moment later another flash of lightning was followed almost immediately by a rumble of thunder, and rain was being blown against the window with more force than ever. The storm seemed almost to be taunting her and trying to warn her that worse was coming.

"Do you remember what I told you about?" she asked Henry. "Do you remember how I warned you about letting the weird noises and... and other weird things get into your head? Well, I have to remember that myself, too. It's so easy for anyone to start letting it all take over and... and seem bigger and more important than it is, when it doesn't really mean anything at all. It doesn't mean a thing, okay?"

Again she waited, but Henry was simply staring at her as if he had no idea what she meant – or, she realized a moment later, as if he thought she was completely out of her mind.

"Stupid phone," she muttered, tossing the phone onto the counter before grabbing some plates so that she could start serving the food. "I should never have bothered, should I? I should have realized that right from the start. Don't worry, Henry, everything's going to be fine. We just... we just have to wait the storm out, that's all. We just have to sit tight and wait for it to go right past us."

CHAPTER TWENTY-SEVEN

WITH HIS BACK TO the wall, Piotr continued to furiously rub the plastic ties against a sharp piece of metal poking out from one of the pipes. So far he hadn't had much luck, but he felt certain that eventually the plastic *had* to break.

"Come on come on come on," he muttered under his breath as he heard another peal of thunder high above the house. "Why aren't you working?"

CHAPTER TWENTY-EIGHT

STANDING AT THE WINDOW in the front room, Julia continued to stare out at the darkness as the storm continued. Every so often the panes rattled or wind blew through the rafters, but she barely reacted at all as she simply watched the darkness of the distant trees.

In some strange way the storm was starting to feel comforting now, as if the rain and wind were conspiring to wrap themselves around the house and keep it separate from the outside world. She was starting to wish that the storm might last forever, although deep down she knew that would be a hellish experience. After all, she was managing to hold herself together so far, but she had no great desire to spend too much time around Henry. At the end of the day, the boy was still a murderer.

If she could be trapped alone with just Ben,

however, that would be entircly different.

Finally, realizing that the television had fallen silent, she turned to see that Henry was sitting on the sofa with the controller in his hands, but that the game had frozen.

"What's wrong?" she asked.

"Nothing," he replied, looking up at her. "I finished it."

"You finished the whole game?"

He nodded.

"So pick another one," she instructed.

"I don't -"

"Just pick another game," she said, more firmly this time. "What's wrong with you? I thought kids your age just wanted to play video games all the time. Ben -"

Catching herself just in time, she silently cursed herself for even saying his name. As she did so, she could already see that Henry was looking down at the floor as if he hated the words that had just spilled from her lips.

"Find a bloody game," she snapped. "Is it that hard?"

Clearly close to tears, he looked at the screen again and began to scroll through the menu. Every few seconds he glanced at Julia as if to check whether or not she was still watching him; she kept her gaze fixed on him firmly, determined to make sure that he was obeying her instructions, until suddenly she heard a heavy bump coming from somewhere above.

"What was that?" Henry asked

"Nothing."

"But -"

"I said it's nothing!" she snarled angrily, before quickly reminding herself that there was no need to panic.

Not yet.

"I'm sorry," she continued, hoping to calm the situation at least a little. "Do you remember what we talked about earlier? This house is always going to make odd noises, especially in bad weather. It's incumbent upon us to make sure that we don't let our imaginations run wild."

"What does... incumbent mean?"

"Don't your parents teach you anything?" she asked, before sighing again. "It means we've got a responsibility to keep our heads together."

Hearing a groaning sound coming from above, as if the very structure of the house was starting to strain under the storm's onslaught, she looked out toward the hallway.

"Just wait here," she added, heading out and making her way to the bottom of the stairs. "I'll just take a quick look for you, okay? But only because I want to put your mind at rest."

CHAPTER TWENTY-NINE

REACHING THE TOP OF the stairs, she stopped and took a look around. She could hear the storm still blasting against the outside of the house, accompanied by occasional high-pitched whistling sounds that suggested the roof could be better insulated, but for the most part the place was holding up well.

Hesitating, she wondered how long she needed to wait before she could convincingly pretend to Henry that she'd searched the entire place.

And then she saw it.

Beyond the open doorway leading into the main bedroom, a figure was standing in the low light. She'd seen this figure before, on her first night in the house, and she felt a shudder pass through her bones as she saw him turning now and stepping out of sight.

"Wait!"

Hurrying over, she looked into the room but saw no sign of anyone.

"I want to talk to you," she continued, keeping her voice low so that Henry wouldn't be able to hear her from downstairs. "I know what you are. I know you're a ghost, you're dead, and that's okay with me. After everything that's happened recently, I don't think a simple ghost is going to be enough to scare me. I'm so far beyond that point, it's almost unreal."

Looking around the room, she still saw no trace of the figure, but she felt sure that she could somehow sense him. Then again, she knew there was a danger that she might be imagining things – and that even the figure itself might have been thrown up by her frazzled brain.

No.

No, she felt sure that she wasn't quite that crazy yet.

"Brian, right?" she said cautiously, hoping to draw the ghostly figure back out. "Was it... Gordon? Brian Gordon? That's you, isn't it? Are you -"

Before she could finish, she heard a brief but distinct bumping sound coming from somewhere over by the other side of the bed.

"I'm not going to hurt you," she explained,

although she wasn't sure she *could* hurt a ghost even if she tried. "I guess people are usually scared of you, right? But the thing is, I already knew that things like you could be real *long* before I set foot in this place. And although I didn't come here specifically to meet you, I'm thinking now that you might be able to help me. There's still so much I don't know and... and that I need to find out."

Struggling to hold back tears, she took a step forward while focusing on the spot just past the headboard. She knew she might be wrong, but she felt that the last bump had come from that very spot.

"I need to know what you can do and... what you can't do. Can you help me work that out? I don't know if you had children when you were alive, but I'm a mother and..."

Her voice trailed off as she realized that she couldn't possibly explain everything. How could she wrap up the events of the previous few weeks in a way that would make any sense to anyone? Even she, who'd lived through it all, was struggling to set it all out neatly.

But she knew she had to keep hold of her sanity.

"I need to know what ghosts are capable of doing," she said softly. "I mean *really* capable of doing, when they're desperate. I need to know what constraints there are and... and what someone might be able to do to stop them. If they were in a tight corner."

Keeping her eyes fixed on the empty spot, she held her breath as she waited for the figure to return.

"If they were really desperate," she added finally, "and they absolutely *had* to make sure that something terrible didn't happen."

She swallowed hard.

"Again."

As the seconds passed, she began to feel as if she was simply being a fool. Slowly, however, the sense of a presence began to grow and now she felt more certain than ever that she wasn't alone in the room. A few seconds later, sensing movement nearby, she turned and saw a shadow moving slowly across one of the other walls. Although it was less distinct than before, the ghostly presence was clearly still nearby.

"Please don't go," she said, raising her voice just a little. "You have no idea how much I need some answers. Not about you, but about..."

Again she wondered how she could ever explain, although she quickly realized that perhaps she needed to try.

"It's about my son," she said finally. "It's about Ben."

Suddenly hearing a bumping sound, she turned and hurried out onto the landing. When she looked down at the hallway, she saw nothing untoward at first, but after a few seconds she realized that the door to the basement was now slightly ajar. Certain that she'd shut it earlier, she hesitated for a few more seconds before racing down, and when she looked through toward the kitchen she saw to her horror that Piotr had escaped and was leading Henry to the back door.

"Stop!" she yelled.

Rushing through, she grabbed Piotr from behind and swung him around, before pushing Henry away and using her body to barricade the door.

"No!" she shouted angrily. "I won't let you take him!"

"This way!" Piotr gasped, grabbing Henry's hand so that he could instead lead him to the front door.

At the last second Julia grabbed the boy's other hand and pulled him back, holding him in place.

"No!" she snapped again. "I won't let you!"

"You kidnapped him!" Piotr shouted breathlessly. "I know who you are! You're that woman who's been on the news, the one whose son died and then you -"

"Shut up!" she yelled.

"You can't be here!" he said firmly. "I'm going to take him to the police!"

"No, not yet!" she sneered, pulling Henry

free before stepping over to Piotr and putting a hand on the side of his arm. "Please, give me a chance to explain," she continued. "I'm begging you."

"Or what?" he asked. "Or you'll knock me out again?"

"I'll sure as hell try," she said, picking up a metal vase from the counter. She paused for a moment but already she was feeling the first flush of anger starting to fade – replaced by desperation. "But only if I have to. Please, can you just give me a few minutes so I can explain everything that's going on here? If you do, I'm certain you'll understand why I'm doing all of this."

CHAPTER THIRTY

"OKAY," PIOTR SAID A couple of minutes later, standing next to the television in the front room as Julia bumped the door shut. "Spill. But don't take too long, because I'm still going to the police when this is all over."

"You're right about who I am," she said as tears began to fill her eyes, glistening in the low light. "My name is Julia Parker, I'm a married woman from Kent."

She hesitated, shocked by how hard it was to state even the simplest of facts.

"A few weeks ago," she continued, "my son Benjamin – Ben – was killed. At school. By two other students from another class who were supposed to be his friends."

"It was all over the news."

"They were playing a game," she explained,

"beyond the reading hut at the end of the schoolyard, and Jacob and Henry had seen a film where some boys killed a monster, and they wanted to act it out. That's what they told the police, anyway. They held Ben down and..."

Her voice trailed off.

"They drowned him, right?" Piotr said after a moment. "That's what they said on the news."

"They claimed they didn't know he'd die," she said softly, as the first tear ran down her face. "They said they thought it was make-believe. I don't know how much I believe them, but in the end maybe it doesn't matter. All that matters is that they..."

She hesitated, before finally bursting into tears as she sat on one end of the sofa.

"Hey, it's okay," Piotr said, struggling to think of anything else to say as he watched her. "I mean, obviously it's *not* okay, but you don't have to cry. Or maybe you should, I don't know. I don't have a clue what it must feel like."

Grabbing some tissues, she dabbed at her eyes.

"Everything is out of control," she sobbed. "I lost my son. He's gone forever."

Piotr opened his mouth to say something, but at the last second he held back. In that moment he felt particularly useless and he was already wondering whether he should simply make for the door.

"They took Jacob and Henry into custody," Julia continued finally. "I don't know how many psychologists they've made them see, but it must be a lot. Because they're so young, there were a lot of discussion about how the case should proceed, but there's no doubt that they did it. They've confessed to the whole thing. They killed my Ben."

"You mean the kid out there, right?" he asked, looking toward the door. "The one in the kitchen. He's one of the ones who killed your son, isn't he?"

Still struggling with tears, she nodded.

"Okay, so what the hell are you doing here with him?" he continued. "He killed your son, so why have you brought him out here to a house in the middle of nowhere? Is it..."

Staring at her, he could scarcely believe the question he was about to ask.

"Is it so you can kill him?" he said finally. "Is it revenge?"

"No," she whimpered, and now her bottom lip was trembling as she shook her head. "Never."

"No-one would blame you," he told her. "And the other boy died, didn't he? The Jacob kid, it was hinted at in the news but people were talking about it online. Something happened to him at whatever facility he'd been taken to."

He waited for Julia to reply.

"Was it you?" he added. "Did *you* kill Jacob?"

Staring at him, she met his gaze for a few tense seconds before very slowing shaking her head.

"Then what the hell's going on here?" he sighed. "I don't get -"

"Ben killed him."

"Ben?"

She nodded.

"Wait," he said after a moment, "I'm confused. I thought... isn't Ben your son?"

She nodded again.

"And Ben's... dead."

"He is."

"So there's another Ben? There's a second Ben?"

"No," she replied. "There's only one Ben in this story."

"You're losing me," he complained, struggling to remain patient. "If they killed Ben, then how can you claim that Ben then killed one of *them*?"

As he waited for a reply, he thought he saw just a hint of a flicker of madness in her eyes. At the same time, he was starting to understand the unspoken point she seemed too afraid to mention.

"Oh... no," he continued. "No, seriously, you can't be suggesting that somehow your dead son came back from beyond the grave and did all of this."

"I'm not suggesting anything," she told him. "I know it's true."

"Listen, I'm sorry about everything you've been through," he replied, holding up both hands. "Truly I am, I can't even begin to imagine what it must be like. Anyone in those circumstances would struggle to hold it all together. Hell, I'm pretty certain that I'd break. Like... my mind would just shatter and I wouldn't even be able to string any sentences together. The fact that you're as sane as you are is a miracle."

Watching her, he realized that she was quietly sobbing once more.

"I don't know what to do for you," he continued, "but I *do* know that the kid in there – whatever he did to your son – needs to be dealt with by the cops. Whatever compelled you to bring him out here, you have to realize that you're not in any fit state to deal with him."

Again he waited for an answer, but he was starting to realize that she seemed to have fallen entirely silent, as if all the manic energy of her endeavor had finally faded.

"So here's what I'm going to do," he went on. "I'm not going to press charges for the stuff you did to me. I won't even mention that to anyone. But I *am* going to take that boy to the police, and then I guess I'll have to tell them how I found him. I'll tell them that you cooperated, though, and I'll try to get them to go easy on you. That's the best I can manage, right? And I'm sure they'll all have a whole lot of sympathy for you. No-one's gonna blame you for... losing the plot slightly. But it's not as if you really hurt anyone."

Turning, he headed toward the door.

"Just sit tight and -"

"Ben killed Jacob," she said suddenly, breaking her silence.

Stopping, he looked back at her – and in that moment he saw so much grit and certainty and determination in her eyes. He could also see that she was struggling to hold herself together and that at any moment she might collapse completely.

"Jacob was one of the boys who drowned him," she continued, "and he was being examined at some facility and they didn't really go into detail but one morning he was found at the bottom of a stairwell and he'd been horribly killed, he'd fallen really far, and from what I heard there's no way anyone could have got him out of his room in the middle of the night and -"

Taking a sudden deep breath, she hesitated for a moment.

"And I had a dream," she explained, "that very night about Ben coming back and looking for revenge, and I realized that he must have been the one who killed Jacob and that he was going to go after Henry next. And I knew that Henry was at a different facility so I just went there and watched the police, and when the chance came I grabbed him and got him away from there because I just figured that hopefully Ben wouldn't be able to find him because the last thing I want – the last thing I can bear – is for my Ben to become some kind of monster."

"I'm sure he's not a monster," Piotr replied, before furrowing his brow. "Wait a moment... do you *actually* think that your dead son came back for revenge as some sort of... ghost?"

"I know he did!" she said firmly, and now her eyes were wider than ever. "I know you probably think I'm insane, but I don't care. When you add my dream to the bits of information I was able to glean about what really happened to Jacob, it's the only thing that makes sense. And I get it, really I do, Ben wants to hurt the people who hurt him and who took him away from me."

"Julia -"

"But I can't let him keep doing it," she stammered, speaking faster and faster now as if she was losing control. "I can't let him be driven by anger and hatred. That's not... that's not my son."

Piotr opened his mouth to reply, but at the last second he realized that she *really* believed everything she'd just told him – and that perhaps it wasn't his job to talk her out of it. As he began to understand the depths of her insanity, he felt nothing but sympathy.

"So I brought Henry here," she added finally, "far away from where Ben can get to him. Because that's how it works, isn't it? Now that we're here, Ben can't find him."

"Ben can't find him because Ben's dead," Piotr replied, hoping that he might finally be managing to get through to her. "That's just a fact."

He felt a huge amount of sorrow for her predicament, but at the same time he knew that somebody needed to step in and end the madness.

"I think you know what has to happen here," he continued. "It's time to take Henry home."

CHAPTER THIRTY-ONE

ALTHOUGH HE COULD HEAR Julia and the strange man talking in the front room, Henry wasn't able to make out any of their words as he sat in the kitchen.

For several minutes now he'd been obediently remaining in the exact space where Julia had told him to wait. He'd tried to escape twice now – once at the service station and once from the house itself – but this time he figured that he needed to be smarter. Even if he managed to get away from the house, he had no idea which way to go; besides, as he looked at the window and saw only darkness outside, he listened to the sound of the storm and he realized that he should probably wait until things calmed down a little.

In the front room, Julia was raising her voice slightly, as if she and the man were arguing.

As much as he wanted to find his family, Henry supposed that he needed to be patient. He looked down at his hands and tried to clean some dirt from under one fingernail, but a few seconds later he froze as he heard a single brief tapping sound at the nearest window.

Turning slowly, he looked at the window and saw only more and more spots of rain hitting the other side of the glass. Beyond the rain, night had fallen.

As he continued to stare at the window, however, he began to feel as if he could somehow sense someone staring at him. He told himself to stop being so foolish, yet the sensation persisted for several more seconds until he felt a desperate urge to duck under the table and hide away. He knew that no-one was supposed to be out there in the yard surrounding the house, although after a moment he began to wonder whether someone might be trying to rescue him.

He glanced into the hallway, just to make sure that Julia was still arguing with the man, and then he got to his feet and walked over to the window. His shadow met him, reflected in the glass, but he tried instead to look past the window itself and to see the yard outside. When that attempt failed, he thought for a moment before crossing the room and using a switch on the wall to turn the light off, and then he advanced toward the window again.

This time he could see outside a little better, and he saw more rain pounding against the glass.

Stopping, he began to wonder what could have caused the tapping sound. The more he stared at the darkness beyond the window, the more he felt certain that somebody was out there. After a few seconds, without really knowing why, he slowly reached up and placed his hand against the cold glass. He waited, telling himself not to panic, but after a few seconds he realized that he could just about make out something shifting in the darkness just a couple of feet beyond the window. Finally, before he had a chance to pull away, he saw another – much paler – hand very slowly emerging from the darkness and touching the window's other side.

Suddenly the lights switched on.

"Hey there," Piotr said, walking into the room. "Henry, how are you doing? Don't worry, Julia told me your name and she and I have been having a little talk, and she's agreed to let me put a plan into action."

Henry continued to stare at the window for a moment, but now he could no longer see the other hand, although he wasn't sure whether this was because of the light or because the person on the other side was gone.

A few seconds later Julia stepped into the doorway, hugging herself tight and sniffing back more tears. As soon as he looked at her, Henry could tell that she'd been crying heavily.

"So here's how it's going to go," Piotr said with a heavily forced smile. "Henry, we're going to take my car to town, and then we're going to see about putting you in touch with your family. Julia realizes that this whole farrago has to come to an end. Meanwhile she's going to stay here and then I'll... come and talk to her again, and we'll figure out where to go from there." He turned to her. "Isn't that right?"

Keeping her eyes fixed on Henry, Julia remained frozen for a second before finally nodding, although she still seemed reluctant.

"So how about that, Henry?" Piotr continued. "Does that sound like a good idea?"

Henry stared at him for a moment before slowly turned and looking at the window again.

CHAPTER THIRTY-TWO

"I REALLY WISH YOU'D come with us," Piotr said a few minutes later as he stood with Julia in the hallway. "I don't like leaving you here like this."

"I'm not going to do anything stupid," she replied, still struggling to hold back tears. "I just... need time to get used to what's happening. It all feels so raw right now."

"I'll probably be gone for about two hours," he told her. "Maybe a little longer, depending on the storm. But I promise I'll come back tonight, and then we'll come up with a plan."

He paused before reaching out and touching the side of her arm.

"I don't think you should be vilified for anything," he continued. "You haven't done anything wrong. Not really. I mean, sure, you kidnapped the kid and there'll probably be consequences for that, but you didn't actually hurt him."

"I slapped him," she admitted tentatively. "At the service station. But only once."

"I think he'll live," he suggested, still touching her arm. "The point is, I'm sure the police will take pity on you. They'll see that you were only trying to do the right thing, and that you didn't hurt Henry even though you had the opportunity."

"I *never* could have done that."

"I know," he replied. "I can tell."

Checking his watch, he looked out at the car and saw Henry sitting in the passenger seat as more and more rain crashed down.

"Can you tell him that I'm sorry?" Julia asked.

He looked at her again.

"When you're away from here, I mean," she continued. "I'm not sure that he'll want to hear it from me again, but please try to make him understand that I was just trying to keep him safe."

"You did a good thing. Even if..."

His voice trailed off.

"It wasn't for him," she added. "Not really. I meant what I said earlier. I was just so scared that Ben would get hold of him and hurt him. I still believe that he killed Jacob, you'll never convince me that he didn't. I can't stand the thought that my son could ever hurt another soul, not even out of revenge."

"Your son -"

"I know what you think," she said firmly, cutting him off. "And I know you're almost certainly right. You have no idea how many crazy thoughts have been going through my head lately, and I suppose I just let some of them take hold of me."

"I still don't like the idea of leaving you here."

"I told you, I'm going to be fine," she insisted. "I'm not going to run off, either. What I did with Henry was stupid and I know I deserve to be punished for it."

Now it was her turn to look out at the car, where Henry was still waiting patiently.

"People probably won't believe me, but I never intended to harm him," she went on. "Quite the opposite, in fact. But I understand how it's going to look, and I'm sure there'll be people who think I had something to do with Jacob's death as well. It'll take a while to clear that all up."

"I'm sure most people will get it," he told her. "Just... maybe don't spend too much time on the internet for a while."

"I need to call my husband and tell him that I'm sorry. Hopefully he'll be able to forgive me."

"I'm sure he will." He put a hand on the side of her arm again. "He must be hurting too. You need each other."

"Get Henry home," she replied, bristling slightly as she pulled away. "Drive carefully. And I'll still be waiting here whenever the police decide to come and find me. I'm sure once I turn my phone on they'll be able to trace me, but it might be quicker if you just let them know what's been going on."

"Everything's going to be fine," he said as he opened the front door and stepped out into the wind and rain. "I promise. No-one's going to judge you too harshly for this. No-one who actually knows what happened, at least."

"I'm sure they'll judge me plenty," she replied, shuddering as she saw him fighting his way to the car, before the front door swung shut and kept the sound of the storm out of the house.

Standing all alone, Julia stared straight ahead and tried to work out exactly how she was going to explain herself when the police finally arrived, and how she was going to make her husband understand. And as lights swung through the darkness outside and a car could be heard driving away, she barely even noticed the sound of something stepping on one of the loose floorboards upstairs.

CHAPTER THIRTY-THREE

"HOW ARE YOU DOING there?" Piotr asked as he eased the car away along the rough road leading to the end of the estate. "Are you hungry? Thirsty?"

"I'm okay," Henry said cautiously, looking around as if he expected to see something in the darkness outside.

"You'll be home soon," Piotr continued. "I'm sure everyone has been very worried about you."

"I don't think they are."

"Of course they're worried. Your parents -"

"My parents don't like me very much," Henry said before he could finish. "Not any more. Not after what Jake and I did to Ben."

"Well," Piotr replied, keeping his attention on the road as he realized that he was in no way qualified to offer advice to a boy in Henry's situation, "there'll be time for all of that to be taken into consideration later."

Reaching the end of the road, he checked for other traffic – a rarity so late, but he knew that occasionally someone might drive past – and then he took a left turn and began to drive toward the distant village. For the next few minutes silence reigned in the car as he told himself that there was really no way he could make small talk with a child, but eventually he worried that the complete lack of conversation was somehow making things worse.

Then again, he had no idea what to say. He tried to imagine what he'd say to one of his own children if they committed such an awful crime, but he couldn't bring himself to get into that mindset. He simply knew that Emily and Harrison were too good, that they could never murder anyone. But if they did – if the unspeakable happened and somehow one of them ever sinned so comprehensively – he wasn't sure that he could ever look them in the eye again.

"It was Jake's idea," Henry said suddenly.

"What do you mean?"

"He's the one who thought it'd be funny to hold Ben under the water," he explained. "We saw it in a game and he said it wouldn't hurt Ben if we only did it for a few minutes."

"And how long *did* you do it for?"

"Longer," Henry admitted, looking down at his hands in his lap. "I thought we should stop but

Jake told me I was wrong and that I was being too soft. And I couldn't do anything because it was really Jake who was pushing on the back of Ben's neck."

"You weren't helping?"

Henry hesitated.

"A little bit."

"Have you told the police all of this? And your parents?"

"I don't think they believe me. I think they think I'm just trying to make excuses."

"You're going to have to live with what you did for the rest of your life," Piotr explained, although he worried that he might be sounding a little too harsh. "There'll be people around to help you deal with it, though. How old are you, again?"

"Ten and a half."

"It'll be okay eventually."

He took the next right turn, and now he was starting to think that silence might be preferable to any kind of awkwardness.

"I thought Ben's mum was going to kill me," Henry said softly, barely getting the words out at all. "I thought that was why she took me out to that strange house."

"She was never going to hurt you at all," he replied, glancing over at the boy again before looking back at the road. "It's complicated but she -"

Suddenly he saw a figure ahead, a young boy picked out in the headlights.

Letting out a cry of shock, Piotr turned the wheel sharply and slammed his foot on the brakes, sending the car racing off the road and slamming into a grassy embankment; the vehicle immediately flipped, rising up for a few seconds into the dark and rainy night before crashing back down onto its roof and sliding to a halt at the edge of the forest with its wheels still spinning and the horn on the steering wheel blaring loudly.

CHAPTER THIRTY-FOUR

SITTING ON A STEP at the foot of the staircase, with her head in her hands as more tears ran down her face, Julia didn't even care that she hadn't moved for a while. After all, there was nothing for her to do, not now that Henry was gone, so instead she figured that she had to simply sit and wait for the police to show up.

Then there'd be handcuffs and questions.

Lots of questions.

She knew she had to try to convince everyone that she'd never meant to hurt Henry. That wouldn't be easy, and she was fully prepared for newspaper headlines to go crazy. At the same time, she felt that she didn't really deserve any sympathy and she figured that spending the rest of her life in jail might actually be an acceptable outcome. After all, what was the point of living now that she no longer had her son?

A moment later she noticed a creaking sound coming from somewhere high above. Turning, she looked up the stairs; at first she saw only darkness on the landing, but after a few more seconds something appeared to shift slightly in the darkness as if a shape was loitering in the gloom.

"Hello?" she said cautiously, getting to her feet. "Is anyone there?"

Remembering Piotr's tale of Brian Gordon, and her own attempt earlier to get through to the ghostly figure, she hesitated before slowly starting to make her way up. Now that Henry was gone, she wasn't even sure that she needed to understand anything about ghosts, but as she reached the top of the stairs she was once again struck by the sense of a nearby presence – this time, however, that sense was impossible to ignore or even to doubt, and she felt quite certain that she was being observed.

"Hello," she said, not using the word as a question this time. "I know there's someone here. My name is Julia Parker, I... I think I told you that already. I was starting to doubt myself earlier, but... you *are* here, aren't you?"

Hearing the faintest shuffling sound, she turned and looked toward the master bedroom. That was where most of the ghostly activity had seemed to happen earlier, so now she stepped over to the doorway with a growing sense of anticipation.

Looking into the room, she saw rain lashing the window as the bed – which she'd made that morning – sat in darkness. And then, very slowly, she began to make out a figure standing on the bed's other side, in more or less exactly the same spot where she'd seen the man earlier. At first she held her breath, not wanting to do anything that might disturb him, but after a few seconds she realized that she needed to try to get through to him.

"Don't be afraid," she said out loud. "Actually, I suppose being afraid should be my job, but the truth is... I'm not. Not of you. You don't strike me as a very mean ghost."

She waited, and she was pleasantly surprised to find that her words didn't seem to be chasing the spectral figure away. A moment later she stepped into the room, and still the figure remained standing by the bed.

Now that she was closer, she could just about make out a few more of the dead man's features. His eyes were set back far into their sockets and she could see heavy shadows marking out his cheekbones. If she'd seen a man like that somewhere else – in the town, perhaps, or in a local pub – she'd certainly have noticed the intensity of his gaze and the thinness of his features, and now she couldn't help but note that he looked very dead, almost as if he'd walked straight out of a mortuary.

And he was staring straight back at her.

"So your name's Brian Gordon, isn't it?" she continued. "Or it was. Well, no, I suppose it still is. Piotr told me the whole story about how you hung yourself in this house. I'm sorry your life ended that way."

She waited for some kind of response, but Brian was still simply staring at her.

"I suppose you're wondering why I didn't scream the first time I saw you," she suggested, "or why I'm not screaming now. The truth is, I've been certain for a while now that ghosts are real. I'm not claiming to understand what it's like to be you, but I *do* have a few questions. They're about my son, mainly. He..."

For a few seconds she wasn't sure she could get the words out.

"He died," she managed finally, and now her voice was filled with emotion as tears returned to her eyes, "and I honestly don't understand what he might be capable of. I suppose that's what I want you to tell me, if you can. Are you here at the house because of some sense of unfinished business? Are you trapped here? If you wanted to leave -"

Suddenly the dead man stepped forward, and Julia instinctively pulled back to keep out of his way as he walked past. She turned to follow him, but in that moment he somehow faded from view.

"Come back!" she called out, hurrying onto the landing but seeing no hint of him now. "I'm really sorry, I didn't mean to scare you off. I just want some answers but... you barely even heard me. Right? You're not just a copy of the man you were before. It's like you're just a reminder of him, a kind of distillation of one important part of who he was."

She paused for a few seconds as she thought back to the sight of his dead eyes.

"But something must be keeping you here," she added. "There must be a reason why some people stay as ghosts and some don't. What exactly is it that makes you stay in this house and wander through its rooms forever?"

CHAPTER THIRTY-FIVE

"WHAT THE -"

Pulling back, and finally allowing the car's horn to stop blaring through the night, Piotr took a moment to pull his senses together. He stared at the cracked windshield, and a moment later he reached up to feel a heavy bruise on one side of his head. A few more seconds passed, however, before he suddenly remembered that he'd been driving with a passenger at the time of the crash.

Turning, he saw Henry hanging unconscious from the seat belts that kept him in position in the overturned car.

"Hey," he stammered, reaching over and shaking the boy gently. "Henry? Wake up!"

Slowly opening his eyes, Henry was clearly dazed as she began to look around.

"Are you okay?" Piotr asked. "Did you hit

your head? Do you think you have a concussion?"

"What happened?" Henry whispered cautiously.

"There was a -"

Stopping himself just in time, Piotr turned and looked out through the cracked window in the door next to him. He saw the bottoms of the trees, and in his mind's eye he was replaying the moment when a young boy had briefly appeared in the middle of the road; the image was so strong that he could scarcely believe it had been real, yet he had no doubt that there'd been *something* out there.

And it had been staring at him, almost as if it had been waiting.

"I didn't hit anyone," he murmured. "I can't have done. I'd have felt it. So the fact that I didn't bump into anything... that means I missed him, right?"

"Where are we?" Henry asked awkwardly.

"Hello?" Piotr yelled, leaning out through the shattered window. "Is anyone there? I'm not mad, I promise, I just... I think we need some help here."

He waited, but he heard nothing until – a few seconds later – Henry began to set out a series of brief gasps.

"Buddy, are you okay there?" he asked, turning to the boy. "Henry, what's going on?"

"Why won't it open?" Henry muttered,

working hard to remove the seat belt.

"I'm not sure you should do that right now," Piotr suggested. "I'm pretty sure that's the only thing holding you to the -"

Before he could finish, Henry let out a cry and dropped down from the seat, landing with a groan against the inside of the car's roof. In the process he accidentally kicked some glass out of the windshield.

"To the seat," Piotr said, before unfastening his own belt. "Actually, you might have a fairly decent plan there. I should probably do the same."

He fiddled with his own belt for a moment before managing to get it loose. As soon as he began to fall from his seat, however, he let out a cry of pain and reached out to steady himself.

"Fuck!" he hissed. "My foot! I couldn't even feel it before but it's..."

He tried again to move, and again he felt only a sharp burning pain.

"It's stuck," he continued, twisting first one way and then the other. "It's kind of a bit numb until I pull, and then..."

Leaning forward, he tried to look down and see exactly what had happened. He strained his neck to get a better view into the footwell but in the darkness he could barely see a thing at all. Reaching around, he tried to find his phone, but somehow in the mess of the crash the damn thing had been lost;

instead he pushed his hand down toward his right ankle, trying to work out how it was pinned, only to freeze as he felt hot blood caked around the opening of his shoe.

"Right," he said after a moment, as he began to realize that the situation was a little more serious than he'd initially understood.

Slowly pulling his hand away from the blood, he made sure to keep it hidden lest the boy might spot any sign of trouble. He knew that even in darkness, blood tended to find a way to make its presence known.

"I'm going to need you to do something for me," he told Henry, and he already knew that this was going to be a big ask. "And it means that you're going to have to be very... *very* brave."

CHAPTER THIRTY-SIX

STEPPING THROUGH INTO THE house's other bedroom, Julia stopped again and listened out for any clue as to the ghost's location. She was far from an expert, but she felt sure that the dead man must still be around – even if, for now, he seemed to prefer to stay out of sight.

The dead had to have rules, she told herself. Just like the living.

"My son is dead," she said after a few seconds, "and I need to know how ghosts work. The truth is, I'm worried he might try to do something bad to one of the boys who killed him. I think he already killed the other boy but..."

Her voice trailed off for a moment.

"I shouldn't have let that guy take him away," she muttered, filling with mounting frustration as she realized that she'd weakened. "I should have stood my ground, but I let him talk me into it. Then again, what if it's not my job to protect anyone? It's not like I -"

Before she could finish that sentence, she felt a flicker of dread in her chest.

"It's not like I protected Ben too well, is it?" she added, once again close to tears. "I wasn't able to protect my own son, so why should I put my life on the line to protect that little bastard Henry?"

As she let the question hang in the air, she realized that she already knew the answer, that she'd rehearsed the answer so many times already and that – despite her inherent cynicism – it was true enough.

"It's because I don't want Ben to become something awful," he said, sniffing back some tears as she looked around the darkened bedroom. "Something vengeful. I pray to God that he didn't hurt Jacob, that whatever happened there was just an accident, and I'm praying again that he won't get to Henry."

Reaching up, she absent-mindedly touched her necklace again, feeling the letters that made up Ben's name. She'd been given the necklace a few years earlier as a gift; it hadn't been anything too expensive, but over the years she'd begun to wear it more and more and now she couldn't remember the last time she'd taken it off.

"He was a good boy," she added. "The best

boy. He didn't have a bad bone in his body and he'd never have hurt another living soul. Not like those so-called friends who drowned him. Believe me, I don't give a damn about either of them, I'd happily leave Henry to rot. It took all my strength to even look at him without feeling sick and without wanting to scream at him but I kept thinking of Ben."

Spotting her own face reflected in the rain-spattered window, she realized that even now she still wanted to scream. But screaming, she quickly reminded herself, wasn't going to achieve anything.

"I just need to be sure," she whispered. "I need to be sure that Ben won't -"

Suddenly she spotted something else reflected in the window, and she realized that she could just about make out a pale face close to her own. Turning, she was shocked to see that the ghostly figure had returned and was slowly making his way out of the room. She had no idea whether her words had encouraged him, but she felt a sense of urgent desperation as she realized that she needed to get through to him.

"Wait!" she gasped, instinctively reaching out to him, only for her hand to pass straight through his arm.

Ignoring her – or perhaps not even noticing her presence at all – the figure stepped out onto the landing.

"That's where you hung yourself!" she called after him. "I know it is! And this is where you always seem to be! Is that what's keeping you here? Are you haunting the spot where you died? You can't help it, can you? This isn't a choice you're making, it's almost like..."

She watched as he approached the top of the stairs, and then she saw that he was looking up at the wooden beams passing overhead.

"It's like you're trapped," she continued, "replaying those final moments over and over. You're not really aware of much, are you? You're like the ghost of a record that's been left on repeat, and you can't break free."

Swallowing hard, she realized that this might be good news.

"You're not *really* Brian Gordon," she said softly. "I mean, you are but... also you're not. You're really just a shell, a remnant of whatever was left of him at the end of his life. Is that what Ben would be if *he* came back as a ghost? Tell me one thing... are you suffering? Are you in pain or... or do you not really know at all?"

She waited, but the figure showed no response at all.

"Tell me!" she shouted angrily, storming forward and trying again to grab his arm. "Tell me how it works!"

Once again her hand passed straight through

him, and this time the figure faded away right in front of her eyes. Left standing alone at the foot of the stairs, Julia turned and looked all around – and now she felt herself filling with rage as she realized that she was being ignored.

"Tell me!" she screamed, determined to get an answer. "I have to know! Tell me how it works!"

CHAPTER THIRTY-SEVEN

STUMBLING ALONG THE DARK road, constantly looking around in case something emerged from the darkness, Henry tried to fight the urge to turn and run away. His eyes were filled with tears and he'd never felt so terrified in all his life, at least not since the police had arrived at the school, but he knew he had to keep walking even as the darkness of the forest threatened to close in on him from either side.

He was soaking wet now from the storm, and almost shivering too as he felt his cold soaked clothes clinging to his skin. More and more rain was falling, battering the ground and causing a monumental hissing sound to rise up all around him in the darkness.

"You have to go back to the house," Piotr had said in the wreckage of the car. "The village is too far away on foot. *Everything's* too far away. So there's really only one option. Since I can't find my phone, I need you to go back there and tell Julia what happened here. Tell her that she needs to call for help."

Those words echoed in Henry's ears now as he reached the turning. Looking along the next road, which somehow was even darker, he knew that the horrible house was waiting a few minutes away. He hated the idea of going anywhere near the place again, and he certainly didn't want to see the woman who'd kidnapped him, but he also understood that the man in the car desperately needed help.

Although Piotr had tried to hide the blood on his hands, Henry had spotted it briefly and he knew that blood meant trouble.

After all, that was why he'd assumed at first that he and Jacob hadn't *really* hurt Ben. There had been no blood, so he'd supposed that Ben was just playing a prank and pretending to be hurt, and that eventually he was going to wake up. In some ways, at the very back of his mind, he still harbored the slimmest of hopes that Ben might still wake up and that everything could go back to normal.

High above, lightning flashed across the sky and thunder soon followed.

"I wouldn't ask you to do this if it wasn't hugely important," he remembered Piotr telling him. "I'm in a bit of a bad way here. There's no need to be scared, you just have to go back along this road and then take the turning that leads to the house. You can do that, can't you? And you might get lucky, another car might come along, in which case you can just tell them instead."

"Okay," Henry had replied. "I'll try."

Still staring at the road leading to the house, he told himself that he could just keep going, that he didn't have to help the man at all. At the same time, part of him wondered whether he might be able to cancel out the bad thing he'd done to Ben. If he helped the man in the car, wouldn't that maybe mean that people wouldn't be so angry at him for everything else?

Looking around, he checked to make sure that he was truly alone and then he set off along the next road. He quickly disappeared into the night as more and more rain lashed down, causing the trees on either side to hiss loudly in the darkness.

CHAPTER THIRTY-EIGHT

"COME ON," PIOTR WHISPERED under his breath, trying to ignore the fact that he felt a little weaker than before. "You can do it."

With his hand reaching down into the footwell, he was feeling the torn part of his sock. Already he could feel fresh warm blood between his fingers; every time he tried to convince himself that the wound probably wasn't too bad, he instead disturbed more evidence to the contrary. His entire right foot was numb now so at least the pain wasn't as awful as before, yet he worried that in the long run that might actually be a bad sign.

Pulling his hand back, he told himself that he should probably just wait for a doctor to show up, although he still wasn't sure that he could entirely trust Henry. The kid seemed a little vacant sometimes, as if he didn't really understand the world, and Piotr worried that even the relatively simple walk back to the house might prove to be too difficult. Then again, with the storm still raging furiously outside, he figured that any kid would struggle to stay calm.

A flash of lightning briefly filled the scene ahead, picking out the windshield's broken glass.

And then, as the darkness returned, Piotr froze as he realized that he'd seen something else. Out there in the forest, about ten feet from the front of the wrecked and overturned car, a figure had been standing between the trees.

Not just any figure, either.

A young boy.

Thinking back to the sight of the boy in the road – the boy who'd caused the car to crash, but whose appearance Piotr had just about convinced himself was an illusion – he immediately realized that it had been the exact same figure.

He stared straight ahead as thunder growled ominously in the sky above. Although he couldn't see anything at all beyond the car now, he was unable to convince himself that the boy had been some trick of the shadows or perhaps an extravagant arrangement of branches.

It had been a young boy.

And he was fairly sure that it wasn't Henry.

"Hello?" he called out now, hoping to somehow prove to himself that he was wrong. "Is anyone there?"

He waited, but the only reply was the constant battering of the rain.

"There's no-one there, right?" he continued. "If there is, could you let me know?"

Reaching past the driver's seat, he once again tried to find his phone, which he still hadn't been able to locate since the crash. He strained to push his hand all the way past the passenger seat, but there was still no sign of anything.

"Henry, is that you?" he asked. "If it's you, I get it. You're scared, but you *have* to go and get help. Do you understand? It's really important."

Straining a little more, he told himself that his phone had to be somewhere nearby.

A moment later, however, he spun around as he heard what seemed to be the sound of footsteps in the mud outside the vehicle.

"Who's there?" he called out, and now he was unable to hide the fear that had begun to seep into his voice.

Waiting for another flash of lightning, he couldn't help but worry that there was something just outside the car. No matter how hard he tried to convince himself that he was wrong, he found himself staring into the darkness and after a few seconds he realized that he was holding his breath.

And then, very slowly, he saw a small pale hand slowly reaching out to touch one edge of the broken window.

"Who are you?" he shouted. "What do you want?"

The hand was resting on the edge now, just about managing to avoid the many shards of broken glass still lodged in the frame.

"What are you doing out in the storm?" Piotr stammered, staring in horror at the hand. "Listen, I don't know who the hell you are or what the hell you're doing here, but I need... I need help, okay? Do you have a phone? Can you call an ambulance? I think -"

Suddenly hearing a ringing sound, he turned and saw that his phone was flashing in the rear of the wreck. Hugely relieved, he reached out and grabbed the device, and when he pulled it closer he saw his wife's name on the screen. Realizing that she was probably worried that he hadn't made it home yet, he tapped to answer.

"Honey," he said, trying to hide the sense of panic in his voice, "I need you to listen to me very carefully. I've been in a crash, I'm hurt and I need to call an ambulance. I'm going to be okay but I need help, so I'm going to cut the call. I just want you to know... I need you to know how much I love you."

"Piotr, what -"

"I have to call an ambulance now," he said firmly. "Honey -"

"You're scaring me," she replied, although

the connection was bad and her voice was already becoming heavily distorted by bursts of static. "Piotr -"

For the next few seconds, all he heard were growls of frantic, hissing noise.

"Honey, listen to me," he continued, hoping against hope that at least she could still hear him. "Everything's going to be just fine but -"

"Why are you getting in the way?" another voice asked suddenly, breaking through the noise coming from the phone. "Why are you here?"

Although he opened his mouth to reply, for a moment Piotr could only stare in horror at the phone as he realized that some other entity was speaking to him now. He quickly tapped to break the call, but the noisy static continued.

"I don't know who you are" the voice continued as the phone's screen began to flicker. "You're making everything harder. Why were you driving him away?"

"Who is this?" Piotr asked cautiously. "What -"

Before he could finish, the phone's screen briefly burned bright white before falling dark again. He tapped at to wake it up again, and then – when that failed to produce a result – he pressed the buttons on the side, but already he could feel that the dead phone was getting hotter and hotter.

A moment later, hearing a dribbling sound,

he turned and looked back into the darkness of the wrecked car. Even about the furore of the howling storm outside, this dribbling sound was now impossible to miss, accompanied by the growing smell of petrol.

"No," he whispered, setting the phone down for a moment as he leaned between the seats. "Please, no..."

As those words left his lips, he realized that he could feel something wet spreading against his torso. He began to pull away, but a moment later the phone jolted back to life, this time with its screen flickering with a kind of strobing gray image of static.

"It's not fair," the boy's voice said again as the device began to emit a series of brief sparks from one side of its casing, and as the smell of petrol became stronger and stronger. "Why do they love him more than they love me?"

"Stop!" Piotr shouted as he saw more sparks emerging from the device. "For the love of -"

Suddenly one of the sparks ignited the spreading petrol, and Piotr could only scream as a wall of fire exploded all around him. Still trapped with one leg in the footwell, he turned and tried to pull away but the flames were already eating away at his flesh. He tilted his head back and tried to scream as his eyes burned and he frantically reached out and tried to find something that he might yet be able to use to save himself. He managed to struggle for several more seconds before the entire rear end of the car exploded, sending the front thudding forward with flames consuming the interior and bursting out through the broken windows. Somewhere in the heart of the inferno, Piotr was still moving for a moment longer before finally he fell still forever.

As the flames continued to burn violently, the figure of a young boy watched from the shadows and then turned to walk away along the road.

CHAPTER THIRTY-NINE

STANDING ON A CHAIR she'd carried up from the kitchen, Julia craned her neck as she tried to get a better look at the wooden beam running above the top of the stairs. She'd noticed that the ghostly figure of Brian Gordon seemed to be endlessly attracted to the landing, and she knew that he'd probably used the beam to tie the rope with which he'd hung himself.

Now, in an attempt to keep her mind occupied while she waited for the police to show up, she was trying to work out exactly what was keeping the ghost in the house.

"There's nothing here," she muttered under her breath as she ran a hand across the rough top section of the beam. "It's just wood."

She wasn't sure exactly what she'd been expecting to find. Part of the original rope, perhaps?

Some other relic of Brian's suicide attempt? Her mind had been racing with all sorts of ideas, none of which had really made much sense, but she knew that the alternative was to sit and do nothing, and that was when the dark thoughts always began to enter her mind.

At least now she could pretend to be busy.

Straining a little harder, she reached toward the very furthest end of the beam. The chair was in danger of toppling now, but in that moment she didn't particularly care: she was far more focused on the task of checking every nook and cranny, and somewhere in the back of her mind she was still convinced that there was some kind of puzzle to be solved, even if she knew she was unlikely to ever -

Suddenly her hand brushed against something softer than wood, and she quickly realized that she'd found a piece of paper. She pulled on it gently, teasing it out, and finally she slipped it out and saw that it was a simple page that had been folded over.

Still standing on the chair, she opened the paper and found a handwritten note.

"Carmen," she read out loud, "I know you won't believe me, I know no-one believes me, but I didn't take that money. They were so clever. They framed me and destroyed my good name. One day the truth will come out, someone just needs to find the Denverdale Lagorcia accounts that were hidden.

I don't blame you for believing them. I love you and the girls so much. Be happy."

She read the note again, trying to make sense of it, and then she looked up once more at the beam. If this had indeed been the spot where Brian had hung himself, then that still didn't explain why he would have hidden the note away in a spot where it was unlikely to be found. She considered the possibility that he'd changed his mind at the last moment and had *wanted* the note to remain unread, but then why hadn't he simply destroyed it?

The only explanation that made even a modicum of sense was that whoever had found the body must have also found the note. Then, perhaps because someone else was around and they didn't want the note to be found, for some reason they couldn't simply put it into their pocket; so they placed it up on the beam instead, and then – in an even more unusual twist – they then couldn't return and retrieve it later. But the note had remained squirreled away ever since, tormenting the ghost of Brian Gordon and keeping his soul tethered to the house.

Once she'd checked that there was nothing else hidden on the beam, she climbed down off the chair.

Sure, she knew her theory about the note was a little desperate and that most likely it could never be proved, but it sort of made sense.

"I found your note,"she said out loud, hoping that she might have been able to give the ghostly figure some degree of closure. "I don't know who Carmen is, but I'll try to find out and... if I can get it to her, or to someone who knows her, then I promise I will. Does that make you feel better?"

She listened, but all she heard was the sound of the storm still battering the house from every direction. And then, a moment later, she heard something else: someone was slowly opening the house's front door. Just as she was starting to convince herself that the wind must be responsible, she heard footsteps.

CHAPTER FORTY

"UPSIDE DOWN?" SHE SAID, shocked by everything Henry had just told her. "But... he's okay, isn't he?"

"I don't know," Henry replied. "He said he couldn't get out of the car. I saw some blood on his leg, I think it was trapped."

For a moment Julia wasn't quite sure what to do with this information. She knew she should call the police, but the whole thing seemed so dramatic that she remained frozen in place for a few more seconds before finally realizing that she had to find her phone.

"Okay, we'll get help," she said, turning to go through to the front room before stopping to look at the boy again. "You're soaked. You must be freezing."

With rainwater dripping from his hair,

Henry shivered slightly.

"Let's grab you a towel," she continued, heading to the hallway, "and then -"

Before she could finish, all the lights flickered off, plunging the house into darkness. Reaching out, she found a switch on the wall and tried it a couple of times, but she quickly realized that all the power was off.

"Great," she said, turning and seeing Henry silhouetted in the kitchen. "Don't worry, I'm sure it's just the storm. It's probably a line that's come down somewhere. There's no need to be scared, I can still find my phone."

She turned to go into the front room, before hearing a sniffling sound. Looking into the kitchen again, she realized that Henry was crying. Her first thought was to go back through and comfort him, but she hesitated as she reminded herself that she had no duty to make the boy feel better. Even the idea of helping him made her feel sick, but on some deeper level she hated the idea that he was suffering. For a few seconds she felt torn between two duties: part of her wanted to help any child in distress, but part of her hated Henry and everything he'd done.

"It's... going to be okay," she stammered, hoping that mere words would be enough. "Just wait here."

Convinced that she'd left her phone up in the

bedroom, she made her way up the stairs. When she reached the dresser, however, there was no sign of the phone at all. She checked the table next to the bed, then she got down onto her knees and felt under the bed, and her mind was racing as she tried to remember exactly where she'd last seen the damn thing. She felt the bed next, and then she got to her feet and made her way carefully out onto the landing.

"It's okay, Henry," she continued, hoping that he could still hear her from downstairs. "I just need to find my phone, that's all."

Next she tried the bathroom, even though she was fairly sure she wasn't going to have any luck in there. Then she made her way into the other bedroom, just to prove to herself that there was no sign of the phone there, either. By the time she emerged onto the pitch black landing again, her mind was racing and she realized that the phone must be downstairs. She couldn't help but recognize the irony: she'd been avoiding the device for a couple of days now, always seeing it but fighting the urge to turn it on, yet now that she actually wanted to find it...

"Come on," she said under her breath. "It's -"

"No!" Henry shouted suddenly, accompanied by a loud bumping sound. "Leave me alone! Go away!"

"What's wrong?" she called out, hurrying down the stairs but finding that Henry was no longer in the kitchen. "Where are you? What -"

In that moment something smashed in the front room. Heading through, she pushed the door open and saw a vase on the floor, and then she stepped past the sofa just in time to see that Henry was trying to crawl into the space behind the armchair.

"What are you doing?" she asked.

"Make him go away!" the boy screamed. "Make him leave me alone!"

"Who?"

"Don't let him in! Lock the door!"

"What are you going on about?" she replied, hurrying across the room and trying to pull the chair aside, only to find that Henry was holding it firmly in place. "Henry, you're freaking out. You need to stay calm."

"He's outside!" he sobbed frantically. "He was looking at me! He was outside at the window and he wouldn't stop staring in at me!"

"Henry, what are you talking about?" she snapped angrily. "Why -"

"It was Ben!" he yelled, glaring up at her with tears running down his face. "Ben's outside! He's come to get me!"

CHAPTER FORTY-ONE

"THERE'S NO-ONE OUT THERE," Julia said a couple of minutes later, standing at the kitchen window and peering out at the darkness.

Rain was still falling against the window but the lightning seemed to have died down a little, at least for now. The wind was howling and various unseen items were shaking and rattling outside, and she knew that someone could easily be in the yard without necessarily being seen, but still...

After a few more seconds, Julia turned and saw that Henry was still standing in the doorway. That was as far as she'd managed to coax him after finally persuading him to venture out from behind the armchair. One thing was certain: the boy's fear was genuine, and she could tell that he wasn't faking anything.

"You probably just saw a shadow," she

continued, even though her heart was pounding. "Listen, I really need to find my phone. Have you seen it? I -"

"It wasn't a shadow," Henry replied, and his voice was extremely tense now. "It was Ben."

"Henry -"

"I know what I saw!" he hissed. "Why won't you believe me?"

"Because Ben is dead!"

As those words left her lips, she felt a shiver run through her bones. In truth, she no longer knew quite *what* she believed. Realizing that she'd begun to fiddle with her necklace, she pulled her hand away as she walked back across the room. She knew she needed to get her thoughts in order, but deep down she still believed that there was a possibility that Ben's ghost might have shown up. Just...

Just not in the house.

Not so far away from where he'd lived and died.

After all, how could he have found them?

"The whole point of coming here," she continued cautiously, "was to get away from... anywhere familiar. Do you understand that? Ben never came within a hundred miles of this house. The idea that his ghost could show up here of all places is crazy. It's nonsense."

"What if he followed us?"

"That's not how it works."

"How do you know?"

"Because ghosts haunt places," she added, "not people."

She knew she had no right to sound so sure of herself, but she figured that she had to cling to her hope that physical distance was enough to keep Henry safe.

"I didn't mean to hurt him," the boy sobbed.

"Let's not talk about that right now," she replied, feeling distinctly uncomfortable. "I need you to help me find my phone so that -"

"I thought it was a game," he added, and now he seemed to be entirely breaking down. "I thought we were just playing. Jake and I played the same game before, just the two of us, and then it was his idea to get Ben to come with us. It wasn't my fault."

"That's... something for the police to deal with."

"Are you sure he's really dead?" he whimpered. "Did they check? Because there wasn't any blood so what if he's just -"

"He's dead!" she snarled, suddenly slapping his face hard. "Don't you get it yet, you little piece of shit? You and your friend murdered my son!"

Stumbling back, Henry bumped against the wall before turning and running. Julia listened to the sound of his footsteps hurrying into the front room, and then she heard some more bumps as he tried again to hide.

"You can't act like you're not responsible now!" she called out to him as she felt her rage starting to overflow. She'd always been able to hold it back before, but not this time; not now that Henry was actively trying to shift the blame for his own actions. "You can't say it's not your fault! What did you *think* was going to happen when you held his head under the water for so long? Are you an idiot?"

She hesitated, before making her way to the hall and then stopping in the door that led to the front room. She could hear Henry sobbing in the darkness but she allowed herself to stay angry.

"I didn't bring you here to absolve you of blame," she sneered. "I didn't bring you here because I want to help you or because I want to save you or anything like that. I brought you here for one reason and one reason only, and that's to stop my son – my Ben – becoming a murderer like you. He might have already killed Jacob, I can't be sure, but I don't want him to turn into some kind of... avenging angel. And he won't, not while we're here."

She waited, but she could still hear Henry weeping over the sound of the storm.

"So if you mistakenly believe that I give a shit about you," she continued, "then you're very wrong. I've hidden my true feelings because I needed to try to get you on my side, but maybe I've been too nice. Maybe I should have kept you tied up the whole time."

She hesitated for a moment before heading back into the kitchen. Grabbing the rest of the supplies she'd used when she'd shoved Piotr down into the basement, she carried them into the front room. She quickly found Henry and pulled him out from behind the armchair; he struggled and shouted, but she held him tight and placed the ties around his wrists and ankles, and then she shoved him down against the floor and tied ropes around his arms.

"There," she continued breathlessly as he sobbed. "Look what you're making me do! Are you happy now?"

"Help me!" he screamed, banging his feet hard against the wall as if he thought someone might hear. In the process, he knocked the video game console onto the floor. "Somebody -"

Before he could finish, Julia shoved the gag into his mouth and pulled tight, securing the straps around the back of his head. He still tried to cry out, but now he could manage no more than a faint muffled groan.

"This is your fault," she hissed into his ear. "You realize that, right? It's your fault that Ben died and it's your fault that we're here and it's your fault that I had to do this to you."

Stepping back, she was just about able to

see him struggling in the darkness. Although Piotr had managed to get free from the basement, she felt certain that Henry wasn't going to be so lucky. She'd already learned so much.

"Maybe I *should* just finish this all right now," she said. "There's no way I can keep us away from the police for much longer. They're going to find us. I came here to think, to come up with a better idea, and now..."

Her voice trailed off for a few seconds as she watched him still squirming.

Suddenly turning and hurrying out of the room, she made her way back into the kitchen. She immediately walked over to the drawers and began to search through them before pulling out the largest knife she could find; holding it up, she saw the blade's edge and tried to work out how quickly she could finish Henry off.

"Everyone'll think that it's just revenge," she whispered, "but it's not that at all. It's just the only way I can think of to get him out of Ben's way. If he has to die anyway, then I'd rather *I* did it. I don't want Ben to be the one who..."

Again her voice trailed off as she slowly turned the knife around.

In her mind's eye, she was imagining herself cutting the boy's throat open. Or might there be a quicker way? She wondered whether simply stabbing him in the heart might be less cruel. She figured that there was no way to kill someone with a knife that wasn't going to be at least a little painful and scary, but she also knew that she didn't have any other options. She didn't want him to suffer, even though she knew she had every right to make him pay; she just wanted him gone, so that Ben wouldn't be tempted to intervene.

And perhaps, deep down, this had always been the plan. Had she just been fooling herself all along?

After a moment she carried the knife back through to the front room, where she found Henry still struggling to get out of the restraints.

"Do you know what a sin-eater is?" she asked. "I do. I've done my research. Sin-eaters conduct certain rituals that they believe allow them to take on the sins of the recently deceased. You'd be surprised how many cultures this concept has cropped up in. There were sin-eaters as far back as human history extends. They didn't want the ghosts of the dead to wander among them, so they took on their sins instead. And in a way, if you think about it, that's exactly what I've been trying to do."

Still holding the knife, she took a step forward.

"Ben was such a good boy," she continued as a tear ran down her cheek. "He was so sweet and innocent and pure. Not like you or your little friend Jacob. Ben was perfect in every way, and then you murdered him. But just because he's dead, that doesn't mean he's not still my son or that I'm not still his mother. And if there's any way at all that I can still protect him, then you'd better believe I'm going to do it."

She adjusted her grip on the knife as she began to realize that she just needed to get on with the task at hand. She just needed to get through one moment of horror, and she felt sure that everything would seem so much clearer on the other side.

"I shouldn't have let that idiot Piotr talk me out of doing the right thing," she added, before slowly kneeling next to Henry and holding the knife up for him to see.

He immediately began to struggle harder than ever.

"Maybe that car crash, or whatever happened out there, was the universe's way of giving me another chance," she sneered as she prepared to plunge the knife into Henry's chest. "That's the way the world works sometimes. They said that Jacob's death was an accident, and maybe that's true. So maybe I still have a chance to stop Ben doing anything bad. I can take on this sin before he has a chance. You have no idea how much I love my son. And if I have to burn for eternity in Hell just to save his soul, then... that's exactly what I'll do."

Henry tried again to cry out, but in that

moment Julia squeezed her eyes tight shut. She took a moment to compose herself, and then – convinced that she was doing the right thing – she plunged the knife down.

CHAPTER FORTY-TWO

"YEAH, I'M ON MY way right now," Julia said several weeks earlier as she drove the car around the corner. "Don't worry, Al, I won't be late. I just -"

Suddenly a figure darted out in front of the car. Letting out a shocked gasp, she slammed her foot on the brake pedal, barley managing to bring the car to a stop in time. Ahead, a young boy on a scooter stopped in the middle of the road and stared at her with a curiously blank expression – almost as if he had no idea how close he'd come to danger.

"What's wrong?" Al asked over the phone.

"I almost hit a kid who shot out into the middle of the road," she sighed as the boy continued on his way.

Winding her window down, she leaned out for a moment.

"Hey!" she called after the boy. "You have

to watch where you're going! And wear a helmet!"

Ignoring her, the boy zoomed away around another corner.

"I don't know why their parents let them go out like that," she said, leaning back for a moment before setting off again, driving toward the school. "He wasn't even wearing a helmet."

"I'm sure it's fine."

"It's not fine, Al!" she hissed. "Are you crazy? When Ben's old enough to go out alone like that and make his own way home from school, he's going to be a hell of a lot more responsible! I don't know what's wrong with some parents these days, it's as if they don't care about their duties."

"You can't stop kids being kids," he replied, sounding amused by her insistence.

"Going out without a helmet isn't kids being kids," she told him. "It's a sign of irresponsible parenting. I know you think I can be too strict sometimes, but I don't care. Ben's not going to grow up as one of those slack kids who constantly get into trouble. He's not going to grow up -"

Before she could get another word out, she spotted flashing blue lights up ahead.

"Hang on," she muttered, "I think something might have happened near the school gates."

Already she could see that the traffic near the school had come to a standstill. After a few more seconds she spotted two ambulances, and a moment later she saw a couple of police cars.

"Something's happened," she added, trying to stay calm. "Al, I'll call you back. I don't know what's going on, but I just need to make sure that everything's okay. I need to find Ben."

CHAPTER FORTY-THREE

"OKAY," DETECTIVE INSPECTOR MCALLISTER said as he watched the technicians assembling next to the body on the grass, "I think you're right. Let's get him moved."

Hearing voices, he turned and looked past the pond, and he saw that several officers were still struggling to contain a growing crowd that was gathering in the school's car park.

"And get uniform to move those people back," he added, making no attempt to hide the disdain in his voice. "What's wrong with them, anyway?"

"Some of them've been trying to film us," Detective Sergeant Henderson replied. "We've told 'em not to, but they just keep going. I don't know what's wrong with people these days."

"Move them well away," McAllister said

firmly as he spotted several officers in a nearby classroom, talking to the two young suspects. "When we move those two boys to the station, I don't want a single soul to see anything. Given their ages, we need to be particularly careful here. I hope I don't need to remind you how this all has to be handled. If anyone in that crowd causes trouble, haul them down to the station and charge them with anything you can think of."

"On it," Henderson said, as he too watched the silhouettes of the two boys for a moment. "I don't get it, though. Those two kids are only ten. How can ten-year-olds commit murder?"

"I'm sure we'll find that the case is a lot more complicated than that," McAllister replied. "Is this the first time you've worked a case involving children?"

"Is it that obvious?"

"You'll get used to it eventually, although I'm not sure that's a good response. The one thing my old boss used to tell me back in the day was that in cases like this, there's often not a simple answer. Human life tends to be messy, and it's not easy to take that mess and set it down in neat little reports with paragraphs and sub-headings. We can only do our best and hope that others do the same, but at the end of the day..."

He paused for a moment, still watching the boys in the classroom.

"Don't try to be perfect," he added. "It's not possible. Just do what you can and -"

Suddenly hearing a voice yelling, he turned and saw that someone had broken away from the crowd and was racing across the grass with a uniformed officer in hot pursuit. After a fraction of a second the uniformed officer tripped and fell, tumbling down as the woman ran closer.

"Ben!" Julia screamed as she stumbled past the edge of the classroom. "Ben, where are you?"

"Damn it," McAllister muttered, turning to Henderson. "You're younger and fitter. Stop her."

Hurrying forward, Henderson grabbed Julia and tried to push her back, but she quickly shoved him aside. Sighing, McAllister then stepped in front of her, and he did a much better job of holding onto her even as she tried frantically to get past.

"Where's my son?" she shouted, watching as the technicians began to lift the covered body onto a trolley. "That's not him! Where is he?"

"Ma'am," McAllister said, struggling to keep her back. "This is a police investigation and an active crime scene, I must ask that you -"

"Someone said it's Ben but it can't be!" she sobbed. "I know it isn't!"

Turning, she saw the two children sitting silhouetted in the classroom.

"Is that him?" she stammered as tears continued to run down her face. "Is he in there?"

"I'm sorry, Sir," the uniformed officer said breathlessly as he finally caught up. "She got a jump on me."

"Ma'am, I need you to go back with this officer," McAllister said firmly. "You absolutely can't be here right now."

"It's not him!" she shouted, as both the officer and Henderson tried unsuccessfully to force her away from the pond. "It can't be him! What are you doing with my son? Where have you taken him?"

"Let's just get you out of here," Henderson muttered. "I think -"

In that moment Julia slammed an elbow into his face, crunching his nose and sending him tumbling back as a stream of expletives fell from his lips. Easily able to get away from the officer now, she raced past McAllister and hurried over to the trolley, where the body was still under a blue plastic sheet.

"I need to see!" she yelled as the technicians tried to push her away. "Let me see him! It's not Ben! Let me see! I have to prove to you that it's not Ben!"

"This is turning into a farce," McAllister hissed as Henderson – with blood gushing from his broken nose – stumbled to his feet. "I'm going to make sure that heads roll for this mess!"

"She broke my nose!" Henderson

stammered. "Did you see that?"

"It'll mend," McAllister said darkly.

"Get out of my way!" Julia screamed, pushing two of the technicians aside with almost inhuman strength as she ran around the trolley and pulled the sheet away. "Get -"

Stopping suddenly, she stared in horror at the pale face of the dead child. She heard voices all around, calling out to her, but she could only look at the boy as her mind tried to find some way to deny the reality of the situation. Finally she told herself that he couldn't be dead, that clearly he was just hurt and that the doctors would be able to help.

"Where are you taking him?" she stammered. "Is he hurt? Is he in a coma? What are you doing? I'm his mother, you shouldn't be taking him anywhere without talking to me first. What happened to him?"

Reaching out, she put a hand on the side of his face.

"Ben?" she continued, horrified by the realization that his skin was so cold. "Wake up, Ben. It's me, it's Mummy, I'm here. Ben, open your eyes. Say something, Ben. What have they done to you? Why are you being like this?"

"Ma'am," one of the technicians said, pulling on her arm, "you really can't be here right now."

"Ben, talk to me!" Julia said, leaning over

him and starting to shake him gently. "Ben, why are you so cold? Have you been in the water? Ben, why aren't you saying anything?"

Reaching down, she forced one of his eyes open, and in that moment she saw that the area around the pupil was filled with blood.

"Ben!" she shouted, as a couple more uniformed officers finally arrived and managed to start dragging her away. "Ben, wake up!"

"Get her out of here," McAllister said, clearly shaken by the entire incident. "Does nobody else here know how to do their jobs? Get this woman out of here right now and find a support officer to talk to her!"

"Ben!" Julia screamed, sobbing frantically as she tried again and again to break free. Already, one of the technicians was placing the sheet back over her son's face. "Talk to me! Ben! What are you doing to my son? Ben! Say something! Ben!"

CHAPTER FORTY-FOUR

THE PHONE RANG AGAIN, shaking slightly as it sat on the car's dashboard.

Staring out the window, watching the drab gray building on the other side of the road, Julia tried at first to ignore the incessant – and highly irritating – buzzing sound. Instead she focused her gaze on the building's front door. A few dried tears could still be seen on her cheeks; in the weeks since her son's death, she'd cried so much that now tears tended to appear in her eyes at seemingly random moments, as if her eyes themselves no longer remembered how to stay dry.

But ever since she'd come up with her plan, ever since she'd finally decided to carry it out, she hadn't felt the same need to cry. The tears were just automatic now, just a nuisance, and she knew that eventually they were going to stop.

Because the plan was going to make everything better.

The plan was going to prove to Ben that she wasn't going to let his killers get away with it.

She'd done her research, following along online, frequenting the deepest and darkest forums and social media pages where people had been discussing the case. While the mainstream media had of course followed all the protocols when it came to reporting on a case involving children, anonymous online sources had been much more open with information. Many of those people had been charlatans, spouting complete nonsense, but she'd gradually learned which ones to trust and she'd figured out the most important information of all.

Jacob Handley was at a police facility in Stevenage and Henry Dartmore was being kept at a different location in Selling.

So close.

It was almost as if the police weren't really trying to keep her away at all.

For reasons of pure geographical convenience, Julia had shown up in Stevenage first. Now she was sitting in her car, watching the front of the facility and waiting for officers to escort Jacob out for a meeting with psychiatrists. She hated how the two murderers were being treated, how they were being coddled and examined when they should be thrown into jail. After all, they were cold-blooded killers and she was certain that they both deserved the most awful punishment. Although she'd previously been against the death penalty, since her son's murder Julia she'd completely changed her mind. Now she wanted Jacob and Henry to hang, or to have them strapped into a chair.

Something.

Anything.

She'd even begun to research medieval execution methods online, trying to find the most painful ways that criminals had been dispatched in the past. The brazen bull had been an obvious favorite, and she'd imagined both Jacob and Henry roasting alive in a metal bull while a baying crowd watched. She'd also liked the idea of public beheading, especially after learning that often the blades used were blunt, meaning that several attempts were required in order to hack the head away. Often the condemned took several minutes to die in agony. She knew she shouldn't want anything like that to happen, but she couldn't help herself.

Someone had to pay for Ben's death.

And if the authorities weren't going to do that, then she was just going to have to take matters into her own hands. The plan was simple enough: kill Jacob and then race to Selling and kill Henry before anyone had a chance to raise the alarm.

Although the timing was tight, she felt sure she could get away with it, at least for long enough to finish the two boys off. After that, she didn't care what they did to her. As far as she was concerned, they could shove her into a brazen bull of her own.

On the dashboard, the phone rang again. She knew it was Al, and she knew he was worried, but she didn't care. Not about Al, not about anything.

Not now.

Glancing down at the seat, she saw the handle of the knife poking out from her bag. And then, just as she was starting to wonder exactly where to aim, she heard the sound of sirens approaching. Looking out the window, she immediately worried that somehow the police were onto her, but a moment later an ambulance raced around the corner and screeched to a halt in front of the building.

For the next couple of minutes, Julia could only stare in confused horror as paramedics raced in and out through the front door. Soon a police car arrived, and she immediately realized that her plan was going to have to be delayed for a day or two.

CHAPTER FORTY-FIVE

"THE INCIDENT IS BEING treated as an accident," Sergeant Draper said as he sat on the sofa in the front room. "A statement will be released to the media, but obviously we won't be going into detail. We won't even be mentioning a name."

"But he's dead?" Al replied, clearly struggling to take in the news. "Jacob's actually dead?"

Draper nodded.

"I don't get it," Al continued. "I thought he was in custody. I thought he was at some... police facility. That's what you told us."

"He was," Draper explained. "I'm not at liberty to go into too much detail, but Jacob has been in police care since the incident at the school. What appears to have happened is that he got out of his room somehow and then he fell over the railing at the top of the staircase. He landed headfirst and although paramedics were called, nothing could be done and I'm afraid he was pronounced dead at the scene."

"How?" Julia asked finally, having been silent for several minutes.

"I'm sorry?"

"How did he fall?" she whispered. "How did he get out of his room?"

"I really can't say," he replied, and it was clear that he was choosing his words with great care. "There'll be a full investigation, we've self-reported to the necessary bodies but these things take time. He seems to have made some claims during the night before his death, and those need to be investigated as well. Obviously the nature of the case means that extra precautions have to be taken. Jacob's parents have been informed and -"

"Fuck Jacob's parents," Julia said, getting to her feet. "They raised a monster. Why should anyone give a damn what they think now?"

"Honey," Al said, reaching out to take her hand, "just -"

"Don't tell me to shut up!" she hissed, pulling her hand away. "What am I supposed to say? That I'm sorry this happened? Because I'm not!"

"Specialist liaison officers are available to help," Draper said as he stood up. "I should get going and leave you to talk, but I believe you have the numbers of -"

"I don't want their help!" Julia snapped. "I want my son back! Can they do that?"

"Thank you for coming today and telling us in person," Al said, standing and reaching out to shake Draper's hand. "We really appreciate that. Why don't I show you to the door?"

As her husband led the officer out of the room, Julia was left standing by the sofa. She could feel the rage and anger starting to ripple through her body and this time she wasn't sure she could keep it all in. In some strange way she felt as if a chance had been snatched away from her; sure, part of her was glad that Jacob was dead but *she* wanted to be the one to kill him. She'd wanted to prove to Ben that she loved him enough to avenge his death, and now that chance had been taken away from her.

Pulling her phone out, she brought up one of the more reliable online forums where people talked about the case. Stepping over to the patio doors, she immediately found that people on the forum were discussing Jacob's death. With a trembling hand, she tapped to open the relevant thread, and then – after scrolling down just a short distance – she froze as she saw comments that had been left by one of the leading sources.

"I work at the place," the man had written. "I'm telling you, the official story's a load of crap.

There's a reason the CCTV from the moment Jacob died has been suppressed. Sure, he fell over the railing, but he wasn't alone when it happened. On some of the frames of the video, you can see an extra shadow next to him and it's obvious he was talking to someone. He was terrified. One of the other guards even reckons he saw it a few hours earlier. Everyone knows the truth: the ghost of Ben Parker led Jacob to those stairs and threw him over the edge."

She read the paragraph several times, and then she scrolled through the various replies. Her initial instinct was to completely ignore the idea of a ghost, yet slowly she felt a sense of dread creeping through her chest. There was one particular poster on the forums who had been right about every aspect of the case so far, and now he was the one claiming that staff at the facility were talking about a strange presence, about a shadowy figure that had seemed to only partially exist.

Was it possible?

Had Ben returned from beyond the grave to get revenge on his killers? Had he got to Jacob before she'd had a chance?

"Honey?"

Startled by a hand touching her arm, she spun around and dropped her phone.

"Honey, are you okay?" Al asked, having evidently returned from seeing Draper out. "Hey, why don't we go for a walk or something? It's not good for us to sit cooped up in here. Or we could call the support team and -"

"I don't want to talk to them," she stammered, before picking her phone up and hiding the screen so that he wouldn't be able to see what she'd been reading. "I hate them. They're idiots."

"Julia -"

"I just want to be left alone," she added, pulling away from him and hurrying to the hallway, then racing up the stairs. "I don't want to talk to anyone. I just want to think. I need to be alone!"

CHAPTER FORTY-SIX

"I DON'T KNOW WHAT'S going on," one of the officers said, stepping back for a moment and looking at the camera above the building's side door.

Holding up a hand, he waved at the camera.

"Should we just go around the front?" the female officer asked wearily, with a hand still resting lightly on Henry's arm.

"No, we can't risk there being photographers," the male officer reminded her, before letting out a sigh. "They were told to expect us. I don't know what these wallies are up to, but I'll go round the front and tell them to open this door. Just wait here, okay?"

As the male officer walked away, his colleague looked down at Henry.

"Just a moment," she told him.

"Am I going to jail?" Henry asked.

"No, you're going to talk to Doctor Phillips again," she replied. "It just has to be here for a change for... operational reasons."

"What does that mean?"

"It means we're going to wait for the door to open, and then we're going to go inside."

She glanced around, watching for any sign of photographers or even just people with cellphones, but so far the scene appeared to be deserted.

"Someone's going to open this door very soon," she added, "and then -"

Suddenly a wooden post slammed into the back of her head, knocking her out cold and sending her body crumpling down to the floor.

Henry immediately turned and let out a shocked gasp, only for Julia to reach down and pick him up.

"If you call for help I'll kill you!" she snarled as she carried him away, hurrying toward her waiting car. "We're going somewhere, Henry. We're going away so that I can help you!"

CHAPTER FORTY-SEVEN

AS HE LOOKED OUT the window a couple of hours later, Henry saw cars racing along the motorway, passing directly beneath the bridge. A moment later, sensing movement, he turned just as Julia took a seat opposite him.

Wearing a baseball cap, she was already glancing around as if she was worried about being recognized. After a few seconds she slid a bottle of cola across the table before removing the lid from her takeaway coffee.

"Drink it," she muttered. "Hurry up. We have to keep moving."

"Where -"

"I've got a place sorted out," she continued quickly, as if she'd anticipated the questions. "It's far but not too far. Everything's planned. Don't worry."

"But -"

"Do you want that drink or not?" she hissed.

Henry hesitated, before taking the plastic bottle and trying to unscrew the cap, only to find that he couldn't quite make it turn. After a couple of seconds Julia impatiently grabbed the bottle from him and pulled the cap away, before shoving it back toward him.

"Drink it," she said firmly. "You know how to do that, don't you?"

Taking a sip from the bottle, Henry couldn't help but notice that Julia was once again looking around as if she expected to be approached at any moment. Although he was struggling to understand exactly what had happened, he knew that Julia was Ben's mother and he really wasn't sure that he was supposed to be with her. He'd heard some of the police officers talking about Jacob earlier and he'd picked up that something bad had happened, and then Julia had knocked the woman police officer out. Now he was starting to wonder whether he should try to run away or ask someone for help.

Glancing around, he saw lots of other people at various tables. There were families of all ages, and a few people eating and drinking alone. Any one of them, he understood, might be able to help – yet they seemed so far away and he was terrified that he might get into even more trouble.

"Okay, let's move," Julia said suddenly,

getting to her feet and grabbing his hand. "We shouldn't have stopped at all. You can drink the rest in the car."

Stumbling as he stood up, Henry had no option but to follow her as she led him away from the cafe area. As he looked around, he saw a news report playing on several television screens mounted to the walls, and his heart skipped a beat as soon as he spotted a photo of Ben. He stopped for a moment, only for Julia to pull him forward just as the picture changed to show her on the screen.

She muttered a few curse words under her breath, but she seemed more interested in talking to herself.

Glancing around, Henry saw people eating and drinking at various fast food places but so far no-one seemed to be paying him any particular attention. He thought about calling out, but he worried that he might only make things worse and a moment later Julia dragged him through a set of doors and into the stairwell leading back down to the car park.

"This way," she said, and their footsteps echoed loudly as they made their way down the steps. "We've got to -"

Suddenly she stopped and pulled back, slamming against the wall with such force that she knocked Henry over.

"What is it?" he asked.

"Please no," she stammered, staring down the steps. "Not now. This can't be happening."

Following her gaze, Henry looked down the stairs but saw nothing other than an advert on the wall promising free drinks with the rewards system at a coffee shop.

"Stay away!" Julia screamed, suddenly grabbing his arm again and forcing him back up the stairs. "I won't let you do it!"

Confused, Henry struggled to stay on his feet as Julia pulled him back up to the double doors. She shoved him through, and then they both stopped as they saw that their sudden return had made enough noise to attract attention. Henry saw several faces staring back at him, and a moment later he looked up to see that the news report was still running.

He saw another photo of Julia, and then he turned to some elderly people sitting at a nearby table.

"Help," he said finally, even though he was terrified of being punished. "Please help me. I've been on the news, I -"

Before he could finish, Julia slammed a hand over his mouth and pulled him back through the doors. Muttering something angrily under her breath, she hauled him up and began to carry him down the stairs, slamming into the wall at one point as she almost fell.

"Stay away from us!" she shouted. "I know what you want but I won't let you get to him! I won't let you become a monster!"

As she reached the bottom of the stairs, she pulled a door open and hurried outside, only to slam Henry's head against the edge. Seemingly not even noticing as he let out a cry of pain and began to cry, she carried him quickly past rows of parked cars while a few shocked onlookers watched.

Nobody intervened, however, and she quickly reached her car and unlocked one of the back doors before shoving him roughly inside.

"We have to get going before they trace the rental details," she said as she hurried back round and clambered into the driver's seat. "Damn it, I knew we shouldn't have stopped. We won't be doing it again."

Sitting up on the back seat as the car's engine rumbled to life, Henry looked outside and saw that several more people had emerged from the stairwell. As the vehicle lurched forward and Julia began to drive toward the exit, the tires screeched and several voices called out telling them to stop, but already the car was speeding out of the service station's car park and onto the motorway.

Almost losing control, Julia just about managed to avoid slamming into the central reservation. After a few more seconds she began to overtake other vehicles while muttering away to herself under her breath.

"It wasn't him," she whispered. "It can't have been him."

Reaching up, Henry touched the side of his head but felt no sign of blood. Looking out of the car, he saw other vehicles flash past just as the engine began to really roar; he'd never been in a car that was going so fast and he couldn't help but worry that they might be about to crash, but he knew that there was no point trying to argue with Julia. Instead he leaned back in the seat and told himself that everything was going to be okay, although part of him worried that he might have missed his last chance to get away.

At the same time, he felt sure that someone must have realized who he was, and that soon his parents or the police would catch up and save him.

"It definitely wasn't him," Julia continued, sounding more and more tense now. "Are you mad? Of course it wasn't him. What would Ben be doing at some rundown service station? You're losing your mind. Keep it together, Julia. You've got to stay calm until you get to the house."

CHAPTER FORTY-EIGHT

STILL KNEELING ON THE floor, Julia stared at the knife's blade and saw that it was embedded a good quarter of an inch deep into the wooden floor. She'd driven it down with such rage and fury, yet at the very last second she'd shifted her aim.

Just a little.

Just enough.

"I can't do it," she whispered, struggling for a moment to pull the blade out before sitting back and looking down at Henry's tied and bound figure. "Why can't I do it?"

As tears streamed down her face, she tried to summon a little more strength. All she had to do, she told herself, was stab the boy one time – and then it would all be over. Ben couldn't possibly hurt Henry if she took care of the little monster first, yet she knew deep down that murdering the child was a step too far. She wanted so badly to stab him in the heart, but after a few more seconds she let out a brief cry of anger as she threw the knife aside and leaned back against the wall.

"Damn it!" she shouted angrily, kicking the side of the sofa. "Why can't I just do it?"

She hesitated, before looking down at Henry and seeing that he was still shivering in the cold. As much as she hated him, she was torn between rage and pity; he was just a child, after all, and she was revolted by the realization that part of her actually wanted to look after him. He and Jacob had ruined her entire world, and she felt as if any slight pang of sympathy was a betrayal of her own son.

Yet as the storm continued to batter the house, she knew she couldn't just leave Henry in such a terrible state.

Grabbing the knife again, she began to cut him free while trying to ignore a sense of nausea.

"You're lucky," she told him breathlessly. "I hope you know that. Anyone else would have killed you by now and they'd be totally justified. I've got every right to gut you like a fish."

As soon as he was free, Henry gasped and pulled away.

"I'm not going to hurt you," she continued, before setting the knife down. "Are you an idiot? If I wanted to hurt you, don't you think I would have done it just now? Believe me, I tried, but I just..."

Her voice trailed off, and after a few seconds she got to her feet and headed over to the fireplace. Grabbing some logs from the pile, she tossed them down before picking up some briquettes, which she placed around the logs before using a match to set fire to the little construction. As the fire began to burn and heat spread through the room, she turned angrily to Henry.

"See?" she snapped as light from the first flames began to dance across one side of her face. "I'm actually trying to help you. I'm sure someone'll be here soon and -"

Before she could finish, she realized that the light from the hearth was just about picking out a small black rectangle on the floor. She stepped over and picked it up, and she realized with a rush of relief that she'd found her phone.

"Finally," she muttered, pressing the button on the side so that she could turn it on. "Don't worry, Henry. Once this thing connects to the network, it won't take long before the police show up. Then they'll take us both away and... I don't know what'll happen to either of us, but we won't see each other again. We'll probably both rot in jail for a while."

"Will I really go to jail?" he whimpered.

"You murdered my son," she sneered, tapping to unlock the phone and then turning to him. "Do you really think you should get away with that, just because you're a child?"

She waited as the phone's home screen appeared, and almost immediately a series of missed calls and unread texts began to arrive, each of them causing the device to buzz. Soon there were twenty missed calls, then thirty, then a hundred and more, while the texts were piling up in the corner. Almost all of the messages were from Al and several were from Jackie, although there were a few from numbers that she could only assume were connected to the police.

Not that the calls or messages mattered, of course.

Setting the phone on the side, she figured that it was probably already serving as a kind of homing beacon. Police cars would be on their way already.

"I'm so tired," she whispered, furrowing her brow. "I just want to sleep and never wake up."

Hearing a scrambling sound, she turned to see that Henry was crawling toward the open doorway.

"You don't have to do that," she told him with obvious pity. "You can walk."

Still on his hands and knees, Henry made his way out into the hall before getting to his feet. Despite the storm still raging outside, *inside* the house a kind of eerie calm had begun to grow and grow, punctuated by occasional creaks and groans coming from high above. Henry stood in the doorway, seemingly not knowing what to do next, and after a few seconds he turned to look back at Julia.

"Go," she murmured. "Stay. Whatever. It'll probably be about fifteen minutes until the police show up, at most. If you're smart, you'll stay here in the dry, but feel free to run out there in the rain and get lost in the big dark forest. I really don't care anymore. I think..."

Pausing for a moment, she stared at the wall.

"I think I was wrong," she added. "Those people on the internet were wrong too. Jacob probably really *did* just fall that night. When I thought I saw Ben on the stairs at that service station, I was probably just losing my mind. And everything here... I'm sure that's just been me breaking down."

She bit her bottom lip for a few seconds as her phone started buzzing again. Someone was trying to call, but she had no intention of answering. Not yet.

They'd find her soon enough.

"I'm a fool," she whispered as fresh tears began to run from her eyes. "I can't prove anything to my son, because my son is dead. He's gone. We haven't even had the funeral yet. You know that, right? He's in some cold locker somewhere, in a coffin, waiting for us to burn him to dust. And that was..."

She continued to stare at the wall, and after a few seconds the phone stopped buzzing again.

"That was supposed to be today," she added softly.

"There's a man on the stairs," Henry said suddenly.

Barely even registering those words, it took Julia a few seconds to turn and look over at him.

"There's a man on the stairs," he said again, taking a step back into the room. "I don't know who he is."

"What are you talking about?" she asked, getting to her feet and wiping tears from her eyes as she stepped past him and looked at the staircase.

She blinked.

"There's no-one there."

"There *was*," Henry replied, turning to look the other way. "He was really angry."

"Well, he's not there now," she pointed out, before flicking the switch on the wall. "The power's still out. We might as well stay near the fire until... until we see flashing blue lights outside."

"But -"

"I don't want to hear it!" she snapped, looking down at him. "You know what? Fine. Do what you want, see if I care. If you want to pretend to see things in the dark, be my guest, just... be quiet about it, okay?"

She stepped back into the front room and made her way over to the fire.

"I'm done," she added. "I -"

"He's right next to you!" Henry gasped, pulling back against the wall. "He's right there!"

"What are you talking about?" she sighed, turning first to her left and then to her right. "You're not even -"

Before she could finish, she saw a figure glaring at her from the shadows. Instinctively taking a step back, she realized that the ghostly figure of Brian Gordon had returned but that this time something was very different; whereas earlier he'd tended to ignore her, now his dead eyes were fixed on her and she could somehow sense a hint of menace emanating from his body. Unable to quite believe what she was seeing, she stared at him for a few more seconds before turning to Henry.

"Get out of here," she said to him, taking a step across the room. "Don't -"

Suddenly one of the chairs lurched past her, slamming hard into the wall. Henry stepped out of the way just in time, and a moment later the chair turned and slid hard into the doorway.

"Climb over it," Julia continued, trying to stay calm.

She took a step toward him, only for several books to fly from the shelves, battering the opposite wall as a few slammed into her shoulder.

Racing past the chair, she grabbed Henry and pushed him into the corner, using her body to shield him as more books flew across the room – followed by a vase that shattered as it hit her in the back.

"Who is he?" Henry shouted. "Why's he so angry!"

"I don't know," Julia replied, looking over her shoulder and seeing that there was once again no sign of Brian Gordon's ghost. She hesitated, but the shelves had been emptied and after a moment she dared to turn around fully. "We just need to get out of here, okay? We're going to get out of the house and let someone else figure out what's going on. Just follow my lead. There's no -"

Before she could finish, she heard a very faint metallic rattling sound. She turned and looked around the room; at first she saw nothing untoward, but after a few more seconds she realized that the sound was in fact several separate noises, and finally she glanced at the fireplace and spotted all four metallic pokers slowly rising up into the air.

She had half a second to react before the first poker spun around and flew through the air.

"Henry!"

Grabbing the boy, she used her own body to shield him as the poker slammed into her back. Letting out a cry of pain, she pulled Henry closer and forced him onto the floor just as the second poker hit her, this time with enough force to make her scream.

The third poker flew straighter, slamming into her spine with its pointed end, but at least now she'd had enough time to brace. She waited for the fourth impact, which came a fraction of a second later and hit the back of her head. Gasping, she immediately reached up and felt blood in her hair.

"We've got to move," she told Henry, figuring that at least there were no more pokers.

Pulling him toward the door, she only managed a couple of steps before two of the heavy metal pokers swung up from the floor and slammed into her face, knocking her back. She managed to hold onto Henry again, pulling him back down, and then she forced him behind the sofa as she heard a loud banging sound filling the room.

"Why does he hate us?" Henry sobbed.

"I don't know that he does," she replied, turning to see that the ghost of Brian Gordon was snarling at her from the shadows. "That wouldn't make any sense. He's more -"

In that moment the ghostly figure rushed at her, grabbing her by the throat and slamming her against the wall.

"Run!" she gurgled, barely able to get any words out at all as she was pulled away and then smashed into the wall again. "Henry -"

As soon as the ghost squeezed tighter, she let out a pained gasp. Trying desperately to get free, she saw the four metal pokers rising up into the air in the middle of the room and slowly turning until their tapered tips were pointing directly at her. She looked down and saw that Henry was still hiding behind the sofa, and in that moment the four pokers all sliced through the air. As Brian Gordon's ghost vanished into thin air, the pokers slammed into Julia's body and she slumped down with sharp pains all over her chest.

Rolling over, she felt blood in the back of her throat. She tried to get up but failed, and a moment later a slip of paper fell from her pocket.

"The note," she stammered, pulling it closer and opening it to see the same spidery handwriting as before.

"I want to go home!" Henry sobbed. "I want -"

Suddenly the entire sofa lifted up and flew back, smashing against the shelves opposite.

"Leave him alone!" Julia yelled, crawling forward to protect Henry with her own battered body. "He's just a child!"

Already she could hear a metallic clanking sound, and she turned to see that the pokers were again being drawn together and lifted up into the air. She took a deep breath and immediately felt a sharp pain in her side, and then – as she looked around for something she might be able to use for defense – she saw the flames still roaring in the fireplace.

"Henry, come with me," she said, grabbing his hand and trying to pull him out of the corner of the room. When he resisted, she turned to him. "Henry, I'm serious! You have to trust me!"

"No!" he cried, slipping his hand away. "Leave me alone!"

Looking back, she saw the ghost of Brian Gordon standing behind the pokers. In that moment, realizing that she had to act, she turned and half ran and half stumbled over to the fireplace. She heard Henry crying out, but she didn't let that distract her as – instead – she reached out and forced the note into the heart of the flames, burning her hand in the process and letting out a scream. Pulling her hand away, she saw the note burning to ash and a moment later an agonized cry rang out across the room.

Turning, she saw the pokers dropping harmlessly to the floor just as the ghost of Brian Gordon faded away and the scream ended.

CHAPTER FORTY-NINE

"IT WAS THE NOTE," she said a few minutes later, putting a blanket around Henry's shivering shoulders as the boy sat on the chair.

Turning to look at the fireplace, where the piece of paper had been reduced to ash, she spent a moment trying to make sense of the last trailing scraps of everything that had just happened.

"He wanted it to be found, but the anger was too much for him. I think the note was anchoring him to the house somehow and he'd lost his mind. The only way to stop him was -"

In that moment, she heard a heavy thumping sound coming from somewhere out in the hall.

"Wait here," she told Henry, stepping away – only for him to reach out and grab her hand.

Looking down, she saw the fear in his eyes.

"I won't go far," she explained, before

checking her watch. "And the police have to be here soon."

She glanced over at her phone and found herself wondering what was taking them so long. She felt sure that they would have picked up her signal by now and that they should be well on their way.

In that moment she heard the thumping sound again.

"I won't go out of sight," she continued, before pulling her hand away and making her way across the room.

She had to pull the sofa and another chair out of the way, but as soon as she stepped out into the hall she looked up the stairs and saw him.

The ghostly figure of Brian Gordon was still in the house, but all his anger and fury appeared to have subsided. She saw his hollow, deathly stare as he loitered at the end of the landing, and then she watched as he turned and drifted silently into one of the bedrooms.

"He's still here," she continued, "but he's gone back to how he was before. Finding the note must have made him stronger, but now that it's gone..."

Her voice trailed off as she realized that the world of the undead seemed to be governed by a number of complex rules. She knew she'd barely scratched the surface when it came to understanding those rules, but she told herself that she didn't really need to figure it all out; the only thing that mattered in that moment was that by destroying the note she'd managed to stop the attack, and she figured that now Brian Gordon's ghost would simply be left to wander the house endlessly.

Either that, or perhaps eventually he might fade away entirely.

Hearing a sobbing sound, she turned to see that Henry was weeping on the chair. Her first thought was disgust, but after a moment – realizing just how much the boy had been through during the ghostly attack – she had no choice; making her way over, she sat down and put her arms around him.

"It's going to be okay," she said softly, before pulling back again. "Just... sit tight."

As those words left her lips, she heard her phone buzzing once more. She turned and saw it vibrating on the table, and she knew that most likely Al or the police were trying to get through, but she couldn't quite bring herself to speak to anyone. Telling herself that they were going to arrive soon enough anyway, she instead got to her feet and headed to the fireplace, where she added a few more logs to the flames.

A moment later the phone fell silent.

She could still hear Henry sobbing, but this time she couldn't quite bring herself to go back and comfort him. He was still, at the end of the day, one of the boys who'd killed her son, and she felt a growing sense of coldness spreading through her chest as she thought back to that day when she'd turned up at the school and had seen a body being removed from the grass next to the pond.

The world had ended in those few fragile seconds.

Her world had ended, at least.

Suddenly her phone started buzzing again. Sighing, she glanced over at it briefly, and then she froze as she saw that something was different this time. As well as vibrating, the phone seemed almost to be changing shape slightly, as if something was shifting on the flat screen. Puzzled, she stepped closer and saw that a small bubble-like protuberance was slowly rising like a blister, while the screen itself showed no name or number calling – simply that someone was trying to get through.

Picking the phone up, she realized that it felt strangely warm. She hesitated, and then she saw that a second blister was forming. Confused, she tapped to answer.

"Hello?" she said cautiously.

All she heard in return was static.

"Hello, this is... this is Julia Parker," she continued. "I'm with Henry Dartmore, I'm in the room with him now and he's fine. I haven't hurt him and I'm not going to, I just... I took him because... because..."

"You're lying," a voice whispered through the static-filled haze.

In that instant Julia felt a rush of shock in her chest as she realized that she recognized that voice. She told herself that she had to be wrong, yet she couldn't deny what she was hearing.

"You were going to hurt Jacob," Ben's voice continued, barely breaking through the line. "You would have hurt him if I hadn't done it first."

"Ben?" she stammered, looking around the room for any sign of her son. "Where are you?"

Nearby, Henry was still sobbing and seemed not to have noticed that Julia was talking to anyone.

"You were going to stab him," Ben explained. "I saw you with the knife. I didn't want you to get into trouble with the police, so I hurt him first. I did it before you went there."

"Ben, no," she said, shaking her head. "That can't be true. Ben, please, you'd never -"

"And now you're going to hurt Henry," he went on, interrupting her. "I don't want you to do that, either. People who do bad things go to bad places and I don't want that to happen to you. Mummy, I hurt the man in the car as well, but that was an accident. I thought he was interfering, I didn't realize he was taking Henry away from you. I thought he was bringing him back."

"Ben -"

"I won't let you hurt Henry," he added. "It's

261

not -"

Before he could finish, the phone suddenly exploded, bursting into flames as the case popped open. As her hand burned, Julia stumbled back and threw the remains down against the floor, and she could only watch in horror for a few seconds as the phone burned brightly. After a moment the brightness began to fade; as a noxious plastic smell rose up from the floor, all that was left of the phone was a melted pile of plastic wrapped around pieces of metal.

Finally the room fell silent again, save for the sound of flames still burning in the fireplace.

"Ben?" Julia said, looking around again. "Are you here? Can you hear me? Ben, if you can hear me, give me a sign."

She waited, and the sense of desperation was growing in her chest with each passing second. Several weeks after losing her son, she felt as if she was on the verge of getting him back again – and she told herself that this time she was going to let nothing keep them apart.

"Ben, I was never actually going to hurt Jacob or Henry," she continued. "At least, I don't think I was. I think I just wanted to try, and I knew I'd fail but I thought in some weird way that I'd be proving something to you. And then when I realized that you might have done that awful thing to Jacob, I wanted to protect Henry from you. I didn't want you to turn into a monster, just like... just like you didn't want *me* to turn into one."

As Henry continued to sob on the chair, she looked the other way.

"We were trying to protect each other," she went on. "But there was no need. Not really. All these plans have been going through my head but now I don't care about any of them. Ben, you're back now and we can be together again. Please, Ben, just let me see you."

She watched the shadows, hoping against hope that he might appear, and a moment later she heard another telltale creaking sound from upstairs. Brian Gordon's ghost was still around, but he was much calmer now and so far there was no further sign of Ben.

"I'm right here," she sobbed as tears filled her eyes. "Ben, come back to me. I'm right -"

In that moment, stopping suddenly, she realized that there was something wrong with the sound of Henry's cries. For minutes now the boy had been weeping on the chair, yet as she slowly turned to him she began to notice that this weeping sound was now more of a frantic, snatching choking gasp.

"Henry?" she whispered, before stepping over to him and looking down at his face. "Henry, what -"

As soon as she saw his eyes, almost bulging

from their sockets, she knew that he couldn't breathe. Reaching up, he was already clutching at his throat and a moment later he rolled over and fell from the chair.

Dropping to her knees, Julia rolled him onto his back and saw his reddened face glaring up at her.

"Ben, no," she stammered, convinced that this was her son's intervention. "Ben, please don't do this. You don't need to hurt him. *I'm* not going to hurt him, so you don't need to either. Please, Ben, you have to listen to me."

Putting her hands on Henry's throat, she realized that she could feel it constricting, as if some unseen pressure was squeezing it from every direction. A moment later the boy grabbed her arm and pulled hard, as if begging her to help, but for a few seconds she realized that she had no idea what to do. As she tried to come up with an idea, she barely even noticed the sound of sirens approaching the house or the flashing blue lights that were looming in the window.

"Ben, stop!" she sobbed as she saw that Henry's eyes were starting to roll into the backs of their sockets. "Ben, I'm begging you, don't do this! You don't have to protect him from me!"

Voices were shouting outside now and after a few seconds someone starting banging hard on the front door.

"Stop!" she screamed, before suddenly reaching up and touching her necklace.

Ripping the necklace away, she held it up and saw her son's name. In that moment, realizing that this might be what had anchored him to her – and that the necklace might even have been the one thing that had allowed him to follow her and Henry all the way to the house – she twisted one side. She had to pull harder, but finally she was able to break the name into two pieces.

"Ben!" she shouted at the top of her voice. "Don't do it!"

In that moment Henry let out a loud gasp before taking in a huge gulp of air, just as several police officers raced into the room and grabbed Julia from behind. As she tried to explain what was happening, they threw her down onto the floor and put her hands behind her back, immediately slapping handcuffs onto her wrists.

"Is he okay?" she yelled over the sound of one of the officers shouting at the others, while another began to tell her about her rights. "You have to help him! Can he breathe?"

Nearby, as the fire continued to burn in the hearth, the necklace's two broken pieces lay unnoticed on the floor.

Amy Cross

CHAPTER FIFTY

"HENRY DARTMORE HAS BEEN sentenced to a youth detention facility," Mr. Seymour said several months later, standing in a corridor in the court building, "and as you heard, the judge has ruled that he needs to be regularly assessed. I'm not going to lie to either of you. It's highly likely that when he turns eighteen he'll be considered for release."

"Even though he killed our son?" Al asked, clearly shocked by the news.

"In general," the solicitor continued, "we don't like to lock children away indefinitely in this country. He'll be given every opportunity to turn over a new leaf. If he shows signs that he might still be dangerous, of course he'll remain locked up. But if he can be rehabilitated, and if he shows remorse for his actions, the system will try to find a way to rehabilitate him and make him useful to society."

"That's ridiculous," Al continued. "He's a -"

"No, it's right," Julia said, interrupting her husband. "He shouldn't pay forever for something he did when..."

Her voice trailed off for a few seconds as she tried to make sense of a rush of conflicting thoughts. Part of her wanted Henry Dartmore to hang for what he'd done to Ben, but she kept telling herself that she had to try to push past her darkest and basest emotions.

"There should always be hope," she added finally, fully aware that those words failed to sum up her feelings very well. "*If* he's genuinely remorseful. But... is there any chance that I could talk to him for a moment?"

"Talk to who?"

"To Henry. I know it might seem unconventional, but I really need to explain why I did what I did. I don't want him to think that I was actually going to hurt him."

"Absolutely not," Mr. Seymour replied gruffly. "Under no circumstances must you ever have any contact with him. Obviously because of his age his identity has been withheld from the media, but we're aware of information circulating online. He'll likely be given a new identity if he's released one day."

"Can I at least get a message to him?"

"I'm sorry, Mrs. Parker, but that's not

allowed either. And it would be a very bad idea."

"I just want him to know that I'm sorry," she continued. "For everything that happened, I mean."

"We need to talk about your own case," he told her. "I'm still confident that the court will show leniency, but it's important that we emphasize the fact that you really weren't thinking straight when you took Henry. The fact that he was mostly unharmed should still be an important factor."

"They'd never send a woman to prison for that, would they?" Al replied. "They wouldn't be that cruel."

"The case is coming up in about a month's time," Mr. Seymour replied as he checked his watch. "Now, if you'll excuse me, I've got another case round the corner this afternoon and I need to grab a bite to eat first. I'll call later in the week to discuss a few matters relating to your next appearance, Mrs. Parker. And for now, I really think you need to try to distract yourselves a little. There's no need to think about young Mr. Dartmore. Not now. His future will be determined by others."

"They won't send you to jail," Al told his wife as the solicitor walked away. "I'm certain of it. They'll understand that you were out of your mind. You weren't responsible for your actions." He placed a hand on her shoulder. "They showed so much leniency for that little shit Henry Dartmore. It'd be insane if they turned around and threw the book at you in a few weeks."

"Maybe," Julia replied, unable to meet his gaze as she instead looked along the corridor, hoping that she might yet get a chance to speak to Henry one last time. "I think I just want to head into town now. Can I meet you at home? There's someone I arranged to meet at a cafe."

CHAPTER FIFTY-ONE

"DENVERDALE LAGORCIA WAS A subsidiary company that handled the estate's farming contracts," Elaine Gordon said as she sat in a seat by the cafe's window. "Granddad didn't have much to do with it, so I don't know whether the investigators would even have paid it any attention at all."

"I'm sorry I don't have the note for you," Julia replied, "but I'm certain that's what it mentioned. Your grandfather seemed to be convinced that the Denverdale Lagorcia accounts would prove his innocence."

"That seems... odd," Elaine admitted, before hesitating for a few seconds as if lost in thought. "I remember Dad saying that Denverdale Lagorcia was the only part of the company that Granddad wasn't allowed much to do with. It definitely bothered him, and toward the end apparently he muttered about it a few times but I didn't really understand. I think I know someone who might be able to help me dig into it a little deeper, though. To be honest, I'd kind of given up on the whole idea of trying to prove his innocence."

She furrowed her brow.

"You said you were led to the note," she added, "but you didn't tell me *how* you were led to it."

"I'm not sure I can explain."

"Did you just stumble onto it?"

Although she wanted to go into detail about everything that had happened at the house, and about her entire experience with the ghostly figure of Brian Gordon, Julia really wasn't sure that she had any proper answers. She hadn't even identified herself as the woman from the news who'd infamously kidnapped her son's killer, and part of her worried that she might accidentally distract Elaine from the task of clearing Brian's name.

"It's complicated," she said finally. "I was out at the house and I sort of... found the piece of paper. It really was a one in a million chance, and then unfortunately the paper fell into the fire. Fortunately I remembered the name Denverdale Lagorcia, though. I just hope that if your grandfather was framed, you're able to prove his innocence."

"It's too late for him, though."

"It's still important," Julia pointed out as she thought back to the ghostly figure in the house. She briefly wondered again whether she should tell Elaine that her grandfather's ghost was still around, but again she worried about the risk of turning the whole situation into a joke.

Getting to her feet, she grabbed her bag.

"I should go," she stammered.

"I'll let you know how this works out," Elaine replied, as she too stood up, "although I've got a feeling that it'll take a while. To start with, I need to talk to the rest of the family and see what they think about the next step. Still, it's the first piece of hope we've had in years so you never know."

"Exactly," Julia said, "and -"

Before she could finish, she spotted a figure standing outside, on the pavement opposite the cafe. Already passersby were blocking the figure, and a moment later they moved out of the way and she saw that the figure was gone. Still, for a few seconds she'd been absolutely convinced that somehow she'd spotted Ben staring straight at her.

"It can't be you," she whispered.

She instinctively reached up to touch her necklace, only to be quickly reminded that it was gone.

"Are you okay?" Elaine asked.

"I'm fine," she replied quickly, trying not to seem flustered even though she worried she was probably coming across as a complete lunatic. Stepping back, she bumped against another table, and she had to apologize to some other customers as she forced herself to stay calm. "I really wish you all the luck in the world clearing your grandfather's name. I'm sorry I can't help with it more, but I'm just someone who found a note. There's nothing else I can do."

With that she turned and hurried out of the cafe, leaving Elaine standing next to the table with a notebook in her hands. Looking down at the words she'd scribbled while talking to Julia, she saw the spot where she'd written the name Denverdale Lagorcia and had then circled it several times. As much as she'd always hoped that her grandfather's name might be cleared, she'd more or less given up on the possibility until now... but Julia's initial message had intrigued her enough to set up a meeting, and she couldn't deny that she was starting to wonder whether her grandfather might in fact have been the victim of a gross miscarriage of justice.

"I'm gonna fight for you, Granddad," she said under her breath as she glanced out the window and saw Julia hurrying away into the crowd. "If someone set you up, I'm gonna make sure they pay. The truth is gonna come out eventually."

CHAPTER FIFTY-TWO

"SO THEN I WAS thinking that we should get away for a while," Al said as he spooled some more spaghetti onto his fork. "It's been so long since we actually took a trip and... I don't know, I'm not sure it's good for either of us to be just sitting around in the house like this. We're like two prisoners waiting for..."

His voice trailed off as he looked past the flickering candle and waited for his wife to respond.

"Honey?" he continued cautiously. "I thought we could try to... move on. I made this romantic dinner specifically to try to get us talking about other things again."

"Other things?" she replied, finally looking up from her plate. "Our son is dead and you think we should try to talk about other things?"

"I didn't mean it like that."

"I can't just forget what happened," she continued, trying to stay calm but increasingly aware that she was starting to lose her focus. "How can you not think about it every second of every day? Al -"

"Of course I think about it all the time," he replied, cutting her off, "but I also know that it's unhealthy to become too obsessed."

"Obsessed?" She slammed her cutlery down. "Does it make me obsessed if -"

Before she could get another word out, something heavy bumped against the floor above. Looking up, she realized that since the kitchen was directly beneath Ben's old bedroom, the sound most likely had come from in there.

"That was nothing," Al said firmly.

"You heard it."

"Something just fell over, that's all," he said, before sighing as he set his fork and spoon down and got to his feet. "I'll prove to you that -"

"I'll go!" she blurted out, scrambling up from the chair and hurrying out of the room, almost tripping over her own feet in the process. "Ben?" she called out. "Are you here? Ben, it's me!"

"You can't be serious," Al said under his breath, taking a moment to listen as he heard his wife still calling their dead son's name out upstairs. "How much longer is this madness going to go on for?"

CHAPTER FIFTY-THREE

"BEN?" JULIA GASPED, HURRYING out of her son's bedroom and then making her way into the office. "Ben, can you hear me? If you're here, let me know. Give me a sign!"

Switching the light on, she stopped and looked all around, but once again there was no sign of him. She waited for a moment longer, however, convinced that eventually he was going to appear. And then, hearing a bumping sound over her shoulder, she spun round.

"Ben, are -"

"It's me," Al said firmly, having followed her upstairs. "Julia, I'm really starting to worry about you. I think the stress of this whole thing is starting to cause some real damage. You need to go and see that therapist again."

"She didn't understand," she replied, turning

to look around the room again. "I could tell she thought I was just being an idiot."

"The court recommended -"

"I don't care what the court recommended," she continued, stumbling over her words a little. "No-one at the stupid court got it either. They all think I'm mad, but I swear it happened exactly as I explained. If they'd just let Henry testify as well, he'd confirm it all."

"You can't seriously expect a court to start believing ghost stories."

"But it's all true!" she snapped, turning to him again.

"It might seem true in your head," he replied, "but you have to recognize that you're not exactly thinking straight. Julia, you've been through so much, it'd almost be stranger if you *weren't* having problems. Do you think I don't feel the same temptation? It'd be so easy to start believing in loads of crazy stuff about ghosts and monsters, but the truth is -"

"That *is* the truth!" she snarled.

"Bullshit!"

Before she could stop herself, she reached up and slapped the side of his face hard. She immediately regretted that move, yet as she stared at his shocked expression she knew there no way she could take it back. She also knew that she was in danger of losing the plot, and that anyone observing her from the outside would undoubtedly have her pegged now as a lunatic, yet she couldn't shake the fear that perhaps Ben's ghost was lingering somewhere and she hadn't noticed. The last thing she could possibly deal with, in that awful moment, was the idea that her son might think he was being forgotten.

"He's here," she stammered, looking all around. "I know you maybe don't sense him, but he's definitely here."

"He's not here, Julia."

She turned to him.

"He's gone," he said firmly. "It's tragic and it's awful, but it's true. Ben is gone and there's nothing we can do to bring him back."

"But I saw him."

He began to shake his head.

"How can you *not* feel it?" she continued, annoyed by the tears that once again were filling her eyes.

"Are you saying that I'm a bad father?" he asked. "A bad father to our dead child?"

"I don't know what I'm saying," she told him, "but I know that he's around somehow. That he came back, and that I had to stop him hurting Henry."

"And are you going to start saying stuff like that in the courtroom?" he replied. "Seriously? Because if you stand up and start going on about ghosts, you're not going to get much sympathy. Then again, you might be written off as having diminished responsibility, so you'd probably end up in a psych ward instead of a prison cell." He stepped closer and put his hands on the side of her arms. "You've been through a lot. We both have. But escaping into some kind of fantasy world isn't going to help either of us."

"But -"

"I need you," he added, looking deep into his eyes. "If we're ever going to get through this, we have to be here for each other. And who knows? Maybe one day soon we can try to have another child."

"You don't get it," she told him. "You don't understand."

"I think a short break isn't going to be enough," he replied. "We need to move away permanently. Away from this house and -"

She immediately started shaking her head.

"I'm being serious," he told her. "There are too many memories of Ben here. Too many reminders. We can't live in the past, so let's move somewhere else. Then, maybe, we can find a way to start again."

"You want to forget him?"

He sighed.

"Do what you want," she said, pulling away and hurrying down the stairs. "We're adults, right?

So we can each deal with this in our own way. We don't have to have a meeting and negotiate a compromise. We can each do our own thing."

"Where are you going?" he called after her. "You're not the only one who misses Ben! I need you! Julia, what do you want right now?"

Stopping at the foot of the staircase, she realized for a moment that she actually wasn't sure how to answer that question. Her first thought had been to simply go to the kitchen, but now she realized that she really just needed to get as far away from the house – and her husband – as possible. Spotting the car keys in a bowl, she grabbed them and slipped her shoes on before marching to the front door and pulling it open.

"Julia, where are you going?" Al asked again, watching her from the top of the stairs. "Are you going to kidnap Henry again? Are you going to do something else that's completely stupid? Why can't you just stay here and be the wife I need right now?"

Ignoring him, she made her way to the car and opened the door. By the time she'd sat down, she already had the seed of a plan in the back of her mind, even if she knew this was a plan that might turn out to be an extremely bad idea. Nevertheless, she started the engine and reversed the car out of the driveway just as Al emerged from the house; she could tell that he was yelling at her, but she quickly swung the car around – narrowly missing a collision with another vehicle that screeched to a halt – and then she began to drive away.

In that moment, she knew exactly where she was going. As if there had ever been any doubt...

CHAPTER FIFTY-FOUR

AS SHE STEPPED OUT of the car, the first thing she noticed was the sense of calm. Somehow, in the space of just a few months, the house in the forest had settled and was now much more tranquil.

More at peace.

Her footsteps trampled across dead leaves as she approached the front door. Somehow, in all the mayhem, she still had a key; and despite her concerns, as she reached the door she saw that the lock hadn't been changed. She saw something else, too, something that surprised her.

"Trevennoray House," she read out loud, from the battered wooden sign above the door. "Huh. It had a name all along."

The key stuck a little in the lock, as if trying to make one last attempt to stop her, but she soon got it to turn. Pushing the door open, she stepped into the hallway and remembered the first time she'd entered Trevennoray House, when she'd had Henry with her.

"Man, it's cold in here," she remembered saying, back when she'd been trying to convince Henry that she'd calmed down after the incident at the service station. "I think I can almost see my breath."

Now the place was entirely dark and gloomy, and had seemingly been shuttered for a few months. She gently pushed the door shut before heading across the hallway, and as she walked upstairs she couldn't help but wonder whether she was making a mistake. At the same time, she wasn't too worried; there was no right or wrong now, just an inexorable march toward something she knew she couldn't avert.

Stopping on the landing, she listened to the silence of the house. Whereas previously she'd been able to easily believe that something unusual was present, now the place seemed empty.

Except...

"Are you here?" she said cautiously. "If you are, I want you to know that I found one of your granddaughters and I told her everything I remembered from the note. I don't know how far she's going to get with it, but at least it's something. And -"

Hearing a bump, she turned and looked into

the master bedroom. After listening for a moment longer and hearing nothing more, she walked to the door and peered into the room.

"The truth always comes out," she added. "That's what I tell myself, anyway. Eventually, one day, your name will be cleared and -"

Suddenly she felt something brushing against her from behind. Turning, she was about to call out again when she spotted just the faintest hint of a shadow moving across the landing and heading toward the other bedroom. Although she couldn't make this shadow out properly, she was just about able to tell that it was indeed the ghost of Brian Gordon, except that he seemed far less present than before.

Less urgent.

Less angry.

Less visible.

"Are you just going to stay here forever?" she asked, just about able to see his dark eyes as he stopped in the doorway. "Is that your fate now? I was hoping you'd have been able to move on, but you're trapped here, aren't you? That must be awful. It must be like... Hell."

She waited, hoping that he might respond in some way and tell her that things weren't so bad, but instead she began to detect a trace of profound sorrow in the dead man. And then, before she had a chance to ask more questions, she watched as he walked into the room; at the same time, his shadow appeared to disappear into the gloom.

"So that's how it works," she whispered, realizing that the worst of her fears had come true. "This is what it means to haunt a place. I can't..."

Her voice trailed off for a few seconds.

"I can't let this happen to Ben," she added finally. "He might still be out there. I made a terrible mistake. I have to set it right."

CHAPTER FIFTY-FIVE

A COUPLE OF HOURS later, as she made her way toward the edge of the lake, Julia felt her phone buzzing yet again. She pulled it out and saw Al's name on the screen, but the battery was already down to just 1% and she was surprised that the damn thing hadn't died already.

Sure enough, a moment later, the buzzing stopped and the screen became dark.

"Sorry," she said under her breath.

She knew she'd have to charge the phone again eventually, but in truth she hadn't really thought more than an hour or two into the future. Not yet. For now, she was content to just go ahead with the scraps of a plan she'd managed to pull together. Having seen the ghost of Brian Gordon one more time, she'd come to understand a little more about ghosts and how they worked, and she understood that sometimes they seemed to become stuck haunting a place.

Or a person.

Now she was at a lake far from home, far from anywhere she'd ever visited before. That was no accident: she'd deliberately sought out a place that had no connection whatsoever to her family, and that she knew Ben had never been near either. She wasn't certain, but she felt this was important not only to cut any ties with particular locations, but also because she needed to prove to herself that her darkest suspicions were correct.

That sometimes ghosts didn't haunt places.

Sometimes they just haunted people.

And she was still a mother, even though her son was dead.

Not gone.

Just dead.

Not an astonishing insight, she realized, but an important distinction that she needed to determine. And so, after a moment's further hesitation, she reached into her pocket and pulled out the two pieces of Ben's name that had previously formed part of a necklace.

Turning the pieces over in her hands, she remembered the moment she'd snapped them apart, and she felt now that she might have been too hasty. At the time she'd been trying to save Henry, and she'd been convinced that she needed to end her son's misery, but now she worried that she might in fact have made everything worse.

What if, in saving Henry, she'd condemned her son to eternity as a haunting presence? What if she'd turned him into a *thing* like the ghost of Brian Gordon?

Realizing that she was delaying the inevitable moment, she pushed the two pieces of Ben's name together, jiggling them slightly until they stuck. She figured that she needed to glue them properly at some point, but for now she found that they stayed together so long as they weren't knocked. Holding them up, she stared at them and waited, although after a few seconds she told herself that she really shouldn't assume that these things worked immediately.

She needed to be patient.

Even if that was the hardest thing in the world.

"I'm here," she whispered finally. "Right here, in a place you don't know. If you come here, I know that it's truly for me and that I'm right. That I'm right about everything."

As a gentle breeze blew across the lake, she kept her gaze fixed firmly on the necklace while feeling a tightening sense of anticipation in her chest. Part of her wanted nothing to happen, in which case she could assume that Ben was finally gone, but another – more insistent – part wanted some sign that he might be able to return, that she might be reunited with her son.

"I'm here," she said again, speaking a little more loudly this time. "I'm waiting for you. All you have to do is give me a sign that you're still around."

In the silence that followed, she felt her sense of certainty starting to slip away. Something about the lake's desolate view made her feel more alone than ever, and she began to wonder whether she was simply going to have to slink home and get on with her monotonous life while waiting for the court date. She was still open to the possibility – no matter how remote – that every supernatural element of her story had been spewed forth by her fevered imagination and that there had never been any ghosts at all.

"I'm right here," she said for a third time. "Sweetheart, please don't be scared. I don't have all the answers, but we can try to figure things out together. Just give me a sign. Anything at all."

Again she waited, and this time she gave him several minutes. Looking down at the necklace again, she began to see it as a petty and insignificant thing, as a sign of her desperation. She let ten minutes go past, then another ten, and then ten more until she knew she'd been sitting in silence for at least half an hour. She wanted to keep calling out to her son, to keep invoking his name, but finally she realized that she had to face facts.

He was gone.

Struggling to hold back tears, she slipped the necklace into her pocket as she turned to walk back to the car. As she did so, she took great care to avoid breaking the name again.

And then, as she took her left hand out of her pocket, she felt another – smaller, and softer – hand reaching out as if from nowhere and giving it a tight squeeze. Letting out a shocked gasp as she stopped, she looked down and instantly recognized Ben's hand, even if it was paler than ever and slightly discolored.

"Mummy," his voice gasped from behind, sounding tight and strained – as if he was struggling to get any words at all out from the depths of his rotten throat. "I'm here."

Also by Amy Cross

The Haunting of Hadlow House: The Complete Series

Beth Cooper is far from happy when her parents announce that they're moving to the countryside. Hadlow House stands just beyond the edge of a small village, and as far as Beth's concerned her life might as well be over. She has no idea, however, that this particular house is home to a number of terrifying ghosts – some of which have been around for more than three hundred years.

Back in 1689, Richard Hadlow was determined to restore his family's name, but a series of tragedies destroyed his plans. Ever since, Hadlow House has been plagued by the ghosts of the lost souls that have died within its walls. Several families have tried to call the house their home, only to fall victim to the horrors that still haunt the property. And every time disaster strikes, another ghost is created.

But why has Hadlow House seemingly been cursed for all these years? Does one ghost lurk further back in the shadows than most, orchestrating everything? And can anyone end the cycle of pain and terror that seems set to never end?

Also by Amy Cross

**Daisy:
The Complete Series**

He kidnapped her. He tied her up in his basement. He prepared to kill her, just like he killed all the others. And then at the last moment he discovered the awful truth... She's the long-lost daughter he never met!

All Daisy Coulson wants to do, after a long day at work, is relax at home. She's heard the news reports about two women who've been murdered in the area, but she's sure she's safe. After all, she's dull and boring, so why would anybody ever want to hurt her? But she's been noticed...

Harry's been killing women for a long time. He doesn't remember any other way of living. It's who he is now. So when he spots an easy target, he doesn't think twice about striking. He soon discovers, however, that there's something very different about his latest victim. Harry's about to uncover a secret that'll change his life forever.

The woman he's kidnapped is the daughter he never knew existed. But he knows now. And she's already seen his face.

Also by Amy Cross

**Wax:
The Complete Series**

All her life, Rachel has wanted just one thing: to meet her mother, the woman who abandoned her as a baby. She's spent many years trying to track her down, and now she has a lead. She travels to the mysterious and remote Harlham Hall, and finally she comes face-to-face with Bernard Cassidy and his wife Evelyn.

Rachel soon realizes that something is very wrong at Harlham Hall. Evelyn seems frail and barely able to remember her life, while Bernard drifts from one broken memory to the next. Strange noises ring out in the house at night and a dark presence lurks in the shadows. Rachel and her boyfriend Brad are reluctant to believe that the house is haunted, but if there are no ghosts at Harlham Hall, what other horror might be waiting in the many empty rooms?

Why did Evelyn give Rachel up all those years ago? What is the terrible secret of Harlham Hall? And what awful bargain did Bernard strike when he first feared that he might be about to lose his wife forever?

BOOKS BY AMY CROSS

42. Raven Revivals (Grave Girl book 2) (2014)

43. Arrival on Thaxos (Dead Souls book 1) (2014)

44. Birthright (Dead Souls book 2) (2014)

45. A Man of Ghosts (Dead Souls book 3) (2014)

46. The Haunting of Hardstone Jail (2014)

47. A Very Respectable Woman (2015)

48. Better the Devil (2015)

49. The Haunting of Marshall Heights (2015)

50. Terror at Camp Everbee (The Ward Z Series book 2) (2015)

51. Guided by Evil (Dead Souls book 4) (2015)

52. Child of a Bloodied Hand (Dead Souls book 5) (2015)

53. Promises of the Dead (Dead Souls book 6) (2015)

54. Days 54 to 61 (Mass Extinction Event book 5) (2015)

55. Angels in the Machine (The Robinson Chronicles book 2) (2015)

56. The Curse of Ah-Qal's Tomb (2015)

57. Broken Red (The Broken Trilogy book 3) (2015)

58. The Farm (2015)

59. Fallen Heroes (Detective Laura Foster book 3) (2015)

60. The Haunting of Emily Stone (2015)

61. Cursed Across Time (Dead Souls book 7) (2015)

62. Destiny of the Dead (Dead Souls book 8) (2015)

63. The Death of Jennifer Kazakos (Dead Souls book 9) (2015)

64. Alice Isn't Well (Death Herself book 1) (2015)

65. Annie's Room (2015)

66. The House on Everley Street (Death Herself book 2) (2015)

67. Meds (The Asylum Trilogy book 2) (2015)

68. Take Me to Church (2015)

69. Ascension (Demon's Grail book 1) (2015)

70. The Priest Hole (Nykolas Freeman book 1) (2015)

71. Eli's Town (2015)

72. The Horror of Raven's Briar Orphanage (Dead Souls book 10) (2015)

73. The Witch of Thaxos (Dead Souls book 11) (2015)

74. The Rise of Ashalla (Dead Souls book 12) (2015)

75. Evolution (Demon's Grail book 2) (2015)

76. The Island (The Island book 1) (2015)

77. The Lighthouse (2015)

78. The Cabin (The Cabin Trilogy book 1) (2015)

79. At the Edge of the Forest (2015)

80. The Devil's Hand (2015)

81. The 13th Demon (Demon's Grail book 3) (2016)

82. After the Cabin (The Cabin Trilogy book 2) (2016)

83. The Border: The Complete Series (2016)

84. The Dead Ones (Death Herself book 3) (2016)

85. A House in London (2016)

86. Persona (The Island book 2) (2016)

87. Battlefield (Nykolas Freeman book 2) (2016)

88. Perfect Little Monsters and Other Stories (2016)

89. The Ghost of Shapley Hall (2016)

90. The Blood House (2016)

91. The Death of Addie Gray (2016)

92. The Girl With Crooked Fangs (2016)

93. Last Wrong Turn (2016)

94. The Body at Auercliff (2016)

95. The Printer From Hell (2016)

96. The Dog (2016)

97. The Nurse (2016)

98. The Haunting of Blackwych Grange (2016)

99. Twisted Little Things and Other Stories (2016)

100. The Horror of Devil's Root Lake (2016)

101. The Disappearance of Katie Wren (2016)

102. B&B (2016)

103. The Bride of Ashbyrn House (2016)

104. The Devil, the Witch and the Whore (The Deal Trilogy book 1) (2016)

105. The Ghosts of Lakeforth Hotel (2016)

106. The Ghost of Longthorn Manor and Other Stories (2016)

107. Laura (2017)

108. The Murder at Skellin Cottage (Jo Mason book 1) (2017)

109. The Curse of Wetherley House (2017)

110. The Ghosts of Hexley Airport (2017)

111. The Return of Rachel Stone (Jo Mason book 2) (2017)

112. Haunted (2017)

113. The Vampire of Downing Street and Other Stories (2017)

114. The Ash House (2017)

115. The Ghost of Molly Holt (2017)

116. The Camera Man (2017)

117. The Soul Auction (2017)

118. The Abyss (The Island book 3) (2017)

119. Broken Window (The House of Jack the Ripper book 1) (2017)

120. In Darkness Dwell (The House of Jack the Ripper book 2) (2017)

121. Cradle to Grave (The House of Jack the Ripper book 3) (2017)

122. The Lady Screams (The House of Jack the Ripper book 4) (2017)

123. A Beast Well Tamed (The House of Jack the Ripper book 5) (2017)

124. Doctor Charles Grazier (The House of Jack the Ripper book 6) (2017)

125. The Raven Watcher (The House of Jack the Ripper book 7) (2017)

126. The Final Act (The House of Jack the Ripper book 8) (2017)

127. Stephen (2017)

128. The Spider (2017)

129. The Mermaid's Revenge (2017)

130. The Girl Who Threw Rocks at the Devil (2018)

131. Friend From the Internet (2018)

132. Beautiful Familiar (2018)

133. One Night at a Soul Auction (2018)

134. 16 Frames of the Devil's Face (2018)

135. The Haunting of Caldgrave House (2018)

136. Like Stones on a Crow's Back (The Deal Trilogy book 2) (2018)

137. Room 9 and Other Stories (2018)

138. The Gravest Girl of All (Grave Girl book 3) (2018)

139. Return to Thaxos (Dead Souls book 13) (2018)

140. The Madness of Annie Radford (The Asylum Trilogy book 3) (2018)

141. The Haunting of Briarwych Church (Briarwych book 1) (2018)

142. I Just Want You To Be Happy (2018)

143. Day 100 (Mass Extinction Event book 6) (2018)

144. The Horror of Briarwych Church (Briarwych book 2) (2018)

145. The Ghost of Briarwych Church (Briarwych book 3) (2018)

146. Lights Out (2019)

147. Apocalypse (The Ward Z Series book 3) (2019)

148. Days 101 to 108 (Mass Extinction Event book 7) (2019)

149. The Haunting of Daniel Bayliss (2019)

150. The Purchase (2019)

151. Harper's Hotel Ghost Girl (Death Herself book 4) (2019)

152. The Haunting of Aldburn House (2019)

153. Days 109 to 116 (Mass Extinction Event book 8) (2019)

154. Bad News (2019)

155. The Wedding of Rachel Blaine (2019)

156. Dark Little Wonders and Other Stories (2019)

157. The Music Man (2019)

158. The Vampire Falls (Three Nights of the Vampire book 1) (2019)

159. The Other Ann (2019)

160. The Butcher's Husband and Other Stories (2019)

161. The Haunting of Lannister Hall (2019)

162. The Vampire Burns (Three Nights of the Vampire book 2) (2019)

163. Days 195 to 202 (Mass Extinction Event book 9) (2019)

164. Escape From Hotel Necro (2019)

165. The Vampire Rises (Three Nights of the Vampire book 3) (2019)

166. Ten Chimes to Midnight: A Collection of Ghost Stories (2019)

167. The Strangler's Daughter (2019)

168. The Beast on the Tracks (2019)

169. The Haunting of the King's Head (2019)

170. I Married a Serial Killer (2019)

171. Your Inhuman Heart (2020)

172. Days 203 to 210 (Mass Extinction Event book 10) (2020)

173. The Ghosts of David Brook (2020)

174. Days 349 to 356 (Mass Extinction Event book 11) (2020)

175. The Horror at Criven Farm (2020)

176. Mary (2020)

177. The Middlewych Experiment (Chaos Gear Annie book 1) (2020)

178. Days 357 to 364 (Mass Extinction Event book 12) (2020)

179. Day 365: The Final Day (Mass Extinction Event book 13) (2020)

180. The Haunting of Hathaway House (2020)

181. Don't Let the Devil Know Your Name (2020)

182. The Legend of Rinth (2020)

183. The Ghost of Old Coal House (2020)

184. The Root (2020)

185. I'm Not a Zombie (2020)

186. The Ghost of Annie Close (2020)

187. The Disappearance of Lonnie James (2020)

188. The Curse of the Langfords (2020)

189. The Haunting of Nelson Street (The Ghosts of Crowford 1) (2020)

190. Strange Little Horrors and Other Stories (2020)

191. The House Where She Died (2020)

192. The Revenge of the Mercy Belle (The Ghosts of Crowford 2) (2020)

193. The Ghost of Crowford School (The Ghosts of Crowford book 3) (2020)

194. The Haunting of Hardlocke House (2020)

195. The Cemetery Ghost (2020)

196. You Should Have Seen Her (2020)

197. The Portrait of Sister Elsa (The Ghosts of Crowford book 4) (2021)

198. The House on Fisher Street (2021)

199. The Haunting of the Crowford Hoy (The Ghosts of Crowford 5) (2021)

200. Trill (2021)

201. The Horror of the Crowford Empire (The Ghosts of Crowford 6) (2021)

202. Out There (The Ted Armitage Trilogy book 1) (2021)

203. The Nightmare of Crowford Hospital (The Ghosts of Crowford 7) (2021)

204. Twist Valley (The Ted Armitage Trilogy book 2) (2021)

205. The Great Beyond (The Ted Armitage Trilogy book 3) (2021)

206. The Haunting of Edward House (2021)

207. The Curse of the Crowford Grand (The Ghosts of Crowford 8) (2021)

208. How to Make a Ghost (2021)

209. The Ghosts of Crossley Manor (The Ghosts of Crowford 9) (2021)

210. The Haunting of Matthew Thorne (2021)

211. The Siege of Crowford Castle (The Ghosts of Crowford 10) (2021)

212. Daisy: The Complete Series (2021)

213. Bait (Bait book 1) (2021)

For more information, visit:

www.amycross.com

Made in the USA
Monee, IL
31 January 2025